Germaine Moreau
and the Mystery
of the Golden Locket

ANNE CROSS

Chapter One: A discovery

Germaine Moreau walked briskly up the steps to her Victorian home, a large book hugged to her chest. She had just been to the Springdale Historical Society's reading room and had borrowed a priceless volume on hand-blocked wallpaper from 1883.

"I have to sketch the design out before I forget it!" she thought as she unlocked the door and set the heavy book down. The talented Germaine Moreau was unlikely to forget anything related to the historical decoration of a home, but she was even modest when speaking only to herself.

After securing the door, Germaine moved into the front parlor and deftly drew the layout of the formal sitting room she'd formulated while walking home from the Historical Society. With the problems of both furniture arrangement and wall covering solved, she breathed a deep sigh of contentment.

She was confident that this was an optimal solution for the room in question. She smiled as she dialed the telephone.

"Hello Mrs. Clovington," she said, "this is Germaine Moreau."

"Oh hello dear," answered Martha Clovington, one of Springdale's most well-known society matrons. "Have you chosen wallpaper that will work in the sitting room?"

"I think so," Germaine answered with her usual understatement. "Several patterns that are authentic to that time period are still in production at a small shop up in Vermont, and there's one with lotus flowers that would be an appropriate match for the Egyptian revival furniture. I've written it all down and I'll bring a sketch and swatches this evening."

"Oh Germaine," Martha Clovington said with pleasure, "I knew you were the right person to help me show off grandfather's old furniture. Who but you would know what to do with that giant sarcophagus? I didn't want to have to put it in storage. You are so clever with these things. I shall see you after dinner, then, dear."

And with that, Germaine Moreau put down the receiver, happy to have been of help. Germaine's interest in the Victorian world started at a very young age. Her parents were historians who had carefully restored the large and comfortable Queen Anne home in which Germaine now lived. As a child, Germaine had learned much about history and the decoration of houses from them and their friends. Mr. and Mrs. Moreau were killed in a rickshaw accident in Shanghai some years ago, and now Germaine lived in the home on her own and continued to research and decorate old houses.

After Germaine put the final touches on the sketch she would later show Martha Clovington, she put down her slender silver pencil and looked towards the back garden.

"Why was dear Miss Rose so adamant about mother and father not changing the rear garden?" Germaine mused, referring to the woman who had owned the house before her parents moved in. "She didn't mind what they did in the front." This was a question she had pondered repeatedly over the past several years, and it came to the fore now that it was spring.

Germaine stared out the window again once more and decided that there was no time like the present to start in the garden. She changed into an outfit of denim jeans and an old work shirt that was once her father's. She found a pair of gardening gloves in the pantry, and rustled around in the old shed for the equipment she would need to get the garden in shape.

Germaine had just begun digging up a large clump of forget-me-nots when she heard the unmistakable "ting" of metal hitting metal.

She put down the shovel and sifted through the dirt to see what it was that she'd dislodged. It took a few moments before she unearthed a large golden locket on a heavy chain. She brushed the surface dirt off and could make out the swirling lines of an engraved monogram. The monogram was so intricately carved that it was impossible for Germaine to decipher the letters. She thought there was an S and perhaps a J, but couldn't be sure. The years' worth of dirt that had lodged in the carving made it even more difficult to read.

Intrigued, she turned the locket over and saw several hallmarks stamped in the gold, but she only knew enough about hallmarks to know that they were European. She was sure the locket opened but didn't want to break it or harm the contents by opening it incorrectly. She turned the piece over and over in her hand until she discovered the lever that would open the mechanism. Before operating the latch, she tucked the locket into her pocket, put away the gardening tools, and went inside. She brought the necklace to the kitchen and very gently brushed off all the dirt using an archeologist's brush that was conveniently located in a pantry drawer. She didn't want any of the dirt to fall inside the locket and ruin whatever secrets the piece might hold. Once everything was clean, she pressed the lever.

Inside were photographs of two women. From the look of their hairstyles and clothing, Germaine estimated the photos to be from the late 1800's and guessed the women might have been in their thirties when the likenesses were made. "But in those days adults all looked about the same age," she thought to herself. The woman on the right seemed taller and thinner than the other but there was something similar about them. "Are they sisters? Cousins? Mother and daughter?" Germaine wondered as she stared at the photos. Both women appeared well dressed and somewhat anxious. Of course, they may have been anxious for the photograph to be completed. It wasn't until around the turn of the century that photographs could be made with a fast enough exposure that the sitters weren't required to stay absolutely still for nearly a minute. Before that development in photographic technology, portraits usually showed very serious faces, like the ones in the locket, because it was nearly impossible to hold a smile for such a long time.

Germaine wanted very much to pry the photographs out from the locket and see if anything was written on their reverse sides, but she knew this might destroy them, so she decided to wait and consult an expert about the miniature photos. Through the years, Germaine had come to know specialists in various fields related to history and antiques, and her winning personality had turned many of these people into good friends. She decided to telephone Dr. Emile Dupre, an expert in nineteenth century photography and one of her college professors, to see if he could shed any light on the photos. She also planned to get in touch with Edward Bartlett of Bartlett's Family Jewels to learn more about the locket itself.

As Germaine closed the locket, she heard a rattling noise. "Oh, I hope I haven't broken the mechanism!" she worried. But the mechanism was sound. She gently shook the locket and realized that the noise was coming from behind the woman's portrait on the right hand side. She got her magnifying glass and saw that there was another almost imperceptible lever on the lip of the piece. She pressed this second mechanism, and the panel holding the woman's portrait sprung open to reveal another compartment.

Inside this compartment was a tiny key on a black silk cord. She picked up the key and saw that the word *"evermore"* had been engraved upon the back of this second, secret part of the locket. Germaine was astonished that the silk hadn't degraded. Germaine was sure that the key was symbolic. The "key to my heart" gesture began in Elizabethan times and was still a token of love today. But her inner sleuth hoped that the key belonged to a lock – a lock that she would be able to discover! "What else might there be in that garden?" she wondered.

But before she could go outside and dig more, Germaine needed to change out of her gardening gear and get her wallpaper samples and drawings together to bring to Martha Clovington's house. Germaine wanted to make sure she kept the locket out of harm's way, so she found a scrap of brocade velvet in her sewing room and quickly created a drawstring pouch that would hold the locket. She placed pouch and contents into a desk drawer in the upstairs library.

As she drove over to the Clovington mansion with her proposal for Martha Clovington's Egyptian Revival room, Germaine kept thinking about the locket and wondering what she would find when she removed the photos. She was mostly able to put the mystery out of her mind as she met with Martha Clovington.

"My goodness, Germaine, this is perfect – and I never would have thought of it," Martha Clovington exclaimed as she looked over the detailed sketches Germaine had prepared.

"Which wallpaper do you prefer?" Germaine asked. "I think the lotus flower pattern gives the room a more feminine feel."

"I agree. And it looks so lovely behind the gilt furniture, the wood seems to glow," replied the satisfied matron.

"Prendergast Paper Hanging does a fine job with these historic papers. If you approve of the plans, I can make all the calls for you tomorrow and the job should be completed before your annual Christmas party," said Germaine, remembering that Martha Clovington hoped to unveil the new sitting room at the large charity gathering she hosted each year.

Mrs. Clovington agreed, and Germaine made her way home with a long list of important phone calls for the next day.

"Who put you in the garden?" Germaine asked the locket, not expecting a response, as she gazed at it one last time before turning in for the night. "And whose initials do you bear?"

Chapter Two: Stop, Thief!

The following morning, Germaine rose early. She sipped her morning coffee and read the newspaper as two loaves of banana nut bread baked in the oven. She hoped that both of the experts she wished to consult would be available to meet with her, and she planned to bring them the homemade treat as a small token of her appreciation. At nine o'clock she called Prendergast Paper Hanging and got Martha Clovington's redecorating business out of the way. Germaine Moreau would never violate the rules of etiquette by phoning anyone before nine o'clock in the morning or after nine o'clock at night. She decided to ring Dr. Dupre next, as she knew Edward Bartlett didn't stray from his shop very often. Dr. Dupre's secretary put her right through to the busy man. Germaine said that she had found an old locket that contained two photographs, and said she'd tell him more in person. Her former professor was intrigued.

"I would love to see what you've found, Germaine, but I am tied up all day today with classes and meetings." he said. "Could you come tomorrow instead?"

"Of course I can," Germaine replied, without revealing her disappointment.

"I'll have one of my best students accompany me, if you don't mind," he went on. "It will be good practice for her. She's almost as good a researcher as you were!"

"Certainly!" exclaimed Germaine. "I remember how helpful it was for me to be able to do real research of this sort when I was in your class. I am so looking forward to seeing you, Dr. Dupre. Until tomorrow, then."

Her next call was to her old friend in the jewelry business.

"Bartlett's Family Jewels," said Edward Bartlett, a bit gruffly, when he answered the phone.

"You'll never believe what this cat dug up in her old garden," Germaine exclaimed.

"Germaine!" he exclaimed, his voice warming. "Let me guess – those gold doubloons that your father stashed under the potatoes?" Edward Bartlett had been a mentor to Germaine's father, and the two had shared numerous adventures and stories about hunting for various antique treasures at auctions and estate sales. Over the years Edward had become like an uncle to Germaine, and his friendship was a great comfort when Germaine lost her parents. Germaine's father, Douglas Moreau, had always had a passion for the Spanish Armada and had often joked about gold doubloons that he'd hidden somewhere for Germaine to find when she was older.

"I had forgotten all about Father's doubloons," said Germaine with a tinge of sadness. "Maybe they'll be my next discovery," she said cheering up a bit. "This is something else entirely. Something more along your line of interest."

"Don't tell me you've found the Angevin diamond!" Edward said, referring to the famous jewel that was stolen from the Tower of London when Eleanor of Aquitaine was the Queen of England.

"Oh, Edward!" Germaine responded with mock exasperation. "Maybe you won't think my discovery is as exciting as the Angevin, but I think it might be just as precious, at least historically. I found an old locket in one of the flower beds at the house. It has a monogram that I can't make out, and there are two photographs inside – both women, and," she went on, "there's a second compartment with a tiny key and another engraving."

"It was in your garden, you say?" Edward asked, his interest piqued.

"Yes, in a flower bed. And I'd like you to look at it. Can I come by today and take you out to lunch?"

"I'd never turn down a chance to spend time with you, Germaine. When will you be here?"

"I have a few things to do here in Springdale, but I could be in Chalmsford at eleven o'clock, if that's not too soon. I'm going to bring the locket to Dr. Dupre tomorrow so he can look at the photographs," Germaine answered.

"So you called the old prof before you called me, eh?" Edward Bartlett joked. "Well at least I get to have a meal with you. Drive carefully, Germaine. Just because your car *can* go ninety miles per hour doesn't mean it has to."

"I promise to obey all posted speed limits," Germaine answered sincerely. And with that, she took another look at the locket, placed it carefully back into its hastily made - yet perfectly executed - velvet pouch and dropped the pouch into her handbag. She hopped into her car and made her way out to Chalmsford.

As Germaine made her way towards that more rural part of the state, she noticed several yard signs promoting Aubrey Bowles, III and Peter Donaghue, both of whom were in the running to be Senator. Jack Ryan had been that region's Senator for many terms. He was popular and effective, but he died at the age of 90 and the governor had called a special election. Although the election was several months away, it was very much in the news. Peter Donaghue had served two terms as governor a decade ago, and had been very effective in keeping the budget balanced while bringing new jobs to the state. He was in his seventies, but Germaine thought that he seemed hale and hearty, like many old Yankees. Aubrey Bowles, III, however, was younger and a newcomer to politics. He was Germaine's age, and had served until recently as the president of Bowles,

Incorporated, his family's business. The company made and serviced some sort of machinery, but Germaine couldn't remember precisely what it was. Aubrey had been a sort of wunderkind, becoming president while he was barely out of his teens. The company had a reputation for ruthless tactics in underbidding competitors. A while back, a worker had been injured at the plant when he fell two stories down an elevator shaft. The worker recovered, but Bowles Incorporated had been reluctant to pay his hospital expenses. Germaine remembered that Aubrey Bowles' brother, Hugo Bowles, had replaced Aubrey as president when the Senate campaign was announced.

Germaine decided she would ask Edward Bartlett more about the Senate race and about the candidates' background over lunch. Edward was usually up on such things. At last, she pulled up in front of Bartlett's Family Jewels. Edward Bartlett had noticed her sporty car drive up and checked his watch. He waved to her from behind the counter as she walked in, jingling the bell that was attached to the door.

"Hello my dear girl!" Edward Bartlett said warmly. "Two hours after we talked – not bad; I hope you didn't speed."

"I promised you I wouldn't," Germaine replied with a mischievous smile.

"Very well, let's see this locket you found. We can catch up over lunch. I've been very curious about this discovery of yours since you called me this morning."

"Here's a little token to thank you for your help," she said as she placed the bread she had prepared that morning on the counter.

"Thank you, Germaine! You know I can't resist your banana bread. I'll tell you whatever you need to know," Edward smiled.

Germaine removed the little velvet pouch from her handbag and showed its contents to her old friend. He turned it over a few times, then took out his jeweler's loupe to get a closer look. He opened the mechanisms, and gently removed the key from the hidden second compartment. He looked at the key with the loupe, and spent several minutes inspecting both pieces before he carefully put them down on a piece of jeweler's cloth.

"It's a beauty, Germaine," said Edward Bartlett, admiring the fine workmanship. "They really don't make lockets like that anymore. Look at this closure. That's all hand worked. They don't even make the tools to create pieces like this anymore." He handed the loupe and the locket to Germaine so that she could appreciate the artistry of the piece.

"I believe the hallmarks are European, but from which country?" asked Germaine, knowing that there were differences in the goldsmithing techniques of each land.

"European. French. Can you guess the maker?" Mr. Bartlett asked.

"Vever? Boucheron? Fouquet?" Germaine asked, listing the few French gold specialists she knew of from the late nineteenth century.

"Boucheron, 1885. Here's the hallmark, and here's the maker's mark," Edward Bartlett said as he pointed to the distinctive Boucheron imprint. But I would guess the person who made the key was Russian. The work on the handle, shaft and bit indicates Russian handiwork. And it seems much earlier than the locket. I would say the key is from the seventeenth century. And it's exquisite."

"My goodness," Germaine exclaimed. "I thought the key was purely decorative, and I thought it was Victorian."

"It is a working key that was probably made for a travelling chest for a noblewoman," said the older jewelry expert.

"Really?" Germaine asked in genuine surprise. "I was sure it was meant to symbolize that the bearer had the key to someone's heart."

"No dear, look here" and with this Edward Bartlett indicated the mechanical nature of the key. "The shaft and bit are much too fine for a simple ornament. Somewhere there is — or at least there *was* — a box with a tiny but very strong gold lock. European noblewomen had to take their jewels with them wherever they went, so they would lock them up in chests. Until about 1703, most locks were so easy to pick that people disguised or hid them to try to foil thieves. But in the early 1600's, a master metalsmith in Siberia figured out how to make an unpickable lock. He was an artist, and he made these locks to be objects of both beauty and use. He had a few apprentices who also learned how to create such locks. They were extremely lovely, and they were extremely strong. Russian goldsmiths were in tremendous demand in all the principalities and duchies of Europe up until the nineteenth century when the aristocracy became less mobile and fixed safes became larger."

"Oh Edward," Germaine said, "I wonder if the box is in the garden? It couldn't possibly be hidden in the house itself; I've been over every inch of the place. My parents used to create scavenger hunts for me, and I'm sure I would have noticed a seventeenth century Russian strongbox. It's all so strange. Why would anyone bury the locket and key in the garden, after all?"

Mr. Bartlett just shrugged. "The heart knows its reasons..."

"...which reason knows not of." Germaine finished the quote with a smile.

"You know, Germaine, I once saw the kind of chest this key might fit and even a locket similar to yours," Edward said, remembering a day long ago.

"Heavens, where? In Russia?" Germaine asked, knowing her friend Edward had travelled widely, with and without her parents.

"Right here in this shop."

Germaine gasped and demanded to know more.

"It was ages ago. I was just a little boy, and I only caught a glimpse of it, but I will never forget how beautiful it was. One afternoon – and I remember it was afternoon because of the golden light that the setting sun cast in the shop – a woman came in to the shop. Very elegant. Very mysterious," he said, in the tone of a seasoned storyteller.

Germaine wanted to question Edward. "Why was she mysterious? What made her elegant?" she wondered. But she knew better than to interrupt her friend when he was telling a story. He would reveal all, as long as she was patient. She bit the side of her tongue to prevent herself from blurting out any questions.

"She was wearing a black veil. In those days ladies still wore hats, and truly elegant ladies wore veils. She was dressed all in black. Head to toe. Hat, veil, overcoat, gloves, shoes. I remember her as quite stylish, not wearing old-fashioned clothes at all," he went on as Germaine bit harder on her tongue.

"She asked my father to lock the door to the shop as she had something very precious to show him, and she didn't want anyone else to wander in. Now mind you, my father was a man who took orders from no one, but this wasn't a lady that a gentleman would refuse, so he did as she asked. As he walked back, she placed one of the most beautiful objects I have ever seen upon the counter. It was resplendent in the afternoon sun – a small gilded chest, inlaid with pearl and lapis lazuli, bound with hammered gold hinges. Germaine, it was amazing. I can see it like it was yesterday, but it must have been a good seventy years ago," Edward said.

"What was inside?" Germaine asked, unable to contain herself any longer.

"Ah, there's the pity," Edward said sadly. "It was so long ago I can't remember anymore. I know my father sent me away. I just don't have a clear memory of anything but that box. She was there for a good long while though. I guess she left with it. Father never mentioned it, and I didn't dare ask. Plus I was a kid, so I soon forgot about it. But years later when I was studying at the metallurgy workshop at the Victoria and Albert

Museum, we read about these chests and I remembered the one I had glimpsed in my childhood."

"That's amazing," she said, admiring her old friend's ability to recall such a thing. "But how can you be sure it was the same sort of box?"

"Oh child, if you had seen it, you wouldn't ask. I'll poke around in some of my old books one of these days and the next time you come to visit, I'll show you what those old Russian jewel chests looked like - unless you find one growing in your garden, and then you can show me," he chuckled.

"Who knows what I'll dig up in that garden," she said with a smile. "I wonder if Miss Rose knew that the locket was there. Maybe that's why she didn't want anything changed. If the locket was Miss Rose's I would certainly like to pass it along to her heirs. I hope I can find out more about it.

"That's also why I want to figure out the inscription. Perhaps it will give me a clue as to whose it was," Germaine said. "Can you make it out?"

"I would say it's an S and a F, but those old inscriptions are deucedly difficult to decipher. However," said Edward

Bartlett, putting the locket down and raising a finger, "I know just the person who could tell us, if you don't mind showing this treasure to one other old antiquer."

"Oh, certainly not. I'd like to show it to as many people as needed to get it to its rightful owner." Germaine said, selflessly.

"Well dear, it's yours by virtue of your ownership of the house. You don't have to give it to anyone," he said.

Germaine looked surprised. "But it's not mine at all. What if it fell off someone's neck when the person was gardening, or what if it was stolen and buried there? This definitely belongs to someone who is not Germaine Moreau," Germaine Moreau said, tapping the locket.

"Maybe the letters read CSB and it was my great-great-grandfather's, in which case you'll have to hand it over to yours truly," Edward Bartlett joked. "The locket and key are worth at least $50,000, Germaine. And if you can identify the photos, it would be worth more. If you came across the chest and it was in similarly good condition, the set would be worth nearly

$100,000. So you may want to reconsider your grand gestures of finding the rightful owner."

"Good heavens!" Germaine exclaimed. "That gives me even more motivation to find whoever this ought to be passed down to. That sort of money could really make a difference in someone's life."

"Well then, let's walk to lunch. We'll stop at Federicka Kroch's on the way and see if she can untangle the monogram. Do you fancy Chinese food?" Edward asked, knowing it was Germaine's favorite and she would say yes.

Federicka Kroch was a German lady who had been living in the United States for many years. She owned a stationer's called The Gilded Nib, and was a handwriting expert. Edward Bartlett knew that she dabbled in monograms and that she would be intrigued by Germaine's valuable locket.

"My dear Frau Kroch, Guten Tag to you!" said Edward warmly as he entered her shop.

"Tag Herr Bartlett" Federicka Kroch replied in lilting Tyrolian inflected English. "What brings you here?"

"My dear friend Germaine Moreau has a mysterious monogram we hoped you could decipher."

"Ah! The charming Germaine Moreau! So nice to meet you, Fräulein. I have heard so much about you from Herr Bartlett," smiled Frau Kroch, extending her hand.

Germaine blushed a little as she reciprocated the handshake.

"And what is the mystery of which you speak?" she asked.

"I found this locket in my garden, Frau Kroch, and I would like to return it to the heirs of the original owner. The former owner of my house was Miss Rose Santini. Although my parents bought the home and all its contents from her just before she died, I think this might have belonged to someone else, because of the initials."

"Ah, so you are as kind and generous as your uncle says! Well, let us see it then. I hope I can help you with this little mystery."

Germaine unwrapped the locket from its velvet pouch and Federicka Kroch let out a low whistle. "Ach, Edward! Why didn't you prepare me? My heart, it will stop! That is not 'a locket' – that is a masterpiece!"

"Federicka used to be an opera singer," Edward said in a loud aside to Germaine as way of explanation for her dramatic tendencies.

"I am choosing to ignore that last statement, Edward," said Frau Kroch as she traced a copy of the monogram onto a sheet of scrap paper.

"These monograms were engraved as a single line," she went on. "To individuate the letters, I must find the starting point, and then trace it. In that way, I can tell what letters are in the monogram."

"How very interesting!" Germaine exclaimed as she watched Frau Kroch's process. "You certainly brought us to the right place, Edward."

"Well Germaine, Frau Kroch can trace the initials and if anyone can trace the owner, I'm sure you can," Edward Bartlett chuckled. "I remember when you were a child you were always poking around your house looking for secret passages and examining things with a magnifying glass; never mind the hours you spent in the library researching whatever caught your fancy. Auguste Dupin and Sherlock Holmes were never far from your mind. You'll get to the bottom of this, I've no doubt."

"I have them," said Frau Kroch at last. "L und S und S again. See here," she said as she pointed to her tracing work.

"L.S.S.," mused Germaine. "I suppose one S could be for Sheppard, but I wonder what the other S and the L stand for? The original owner of my house was Lyman Sheppard, Miss Rose's maternal grandfather, but this is a woman's piece of jewelry." Germaine's curiosity was even further piqued.

"Frau Kroch," she asked respectfully, "does the order of the letters have any significance? Would the surname always appear in the middle?"

"Yah," she answered. "In that time, this is Victorian, high Victorian, the initials on such a fancy piece of jewelry would have been Christian name, Family name, then Middle Initial or Maiden name if the wearer was married. This era was very tradition-minded, and social customs were very important. Using the wrong initial order would have been very bohemian, and unlikely for someone wearing the solid gold Boucheron."

"Well this is a big help, Frau Kroch. Thank you so much for your time. Now at least I have the right initials to go on. It's a start!"

"You're welcome Miss Moreau. It's a pleasure even to see such a beautiful old piece of jewelry. Maybe you will keep it and wear it? At least I hope you will come and say hello the next time you visit your uncle!"

"Oh I surely will!" Germaine responded, making a mental note to send a special bouquet of flowers to Frau Kroch to thank her for her help as soon as she returned home.

Edward Bartlett and Germaine Moreau took leave of Frau Kroch, and headed across the Chalmsford town green to the Floating Pagoda, Germaine's favorite Chinese restaurant. Germaine laced her left arm through Edward's and adjusted her handbag to her right hand. As they crossed the street, she was jostled by someone behind her, and began to stumble. As she attempted to regain her balance, she felt a tug at her purse and in the next instant it was gone. She watched in horror as an unknown man ran down the street with her handbag clutched to his chest.

"Stop, thief!" Germaine yelled to the passersby. "That man stole my handbag – stop him!"

Chapter Three: An ominous fortune

Germaine let go of Edward's arm and began to run as quickly as she could after the culprit, yelling "Help, help!" as she went.

Although many people turned and looked, no one seemed interested in intervening. "He stole my bag! Stop him!" Germaine yelled, in mounting desperation, with the purse snatcher still in sight.

Eventually the thief and his pursuer came to a crowded intersection undergoing road repairs. A police officer was standing in the street directing traffic. "Officer! That man stole my purse!" Germaine yelled, with the last bit of air in her lungs. The policeman didn't seem to hear her over the din of traffic and construction, but he could certainly tell that something was wrong. The thief must have figured the gig was up, as he threw Germaine's purse into the traffic and ran in the opposite direction.

"The locket, the locket!" Germaine fretted as she made her way through the traffic. "Oh what will I do if one of these cars runs over my purse?" she worried.

But the policeman finally realized what had happened and stopped the traffic in all directions. Germaine was able to reach her bag safely and then made her way over to a park bench to examine its contents and regain her breath.

"Are you alright miss?" asked the officer who had come to her side.

"Yes, officer, I'm alright." Germaine responded as she looked through her bag, desperate to find the locket.

"That man didn't assault you?" he went on.

"Oh, no, he just pushed me, and when I lost my balance, he grabbed my purse. I suppose it was a little careless of me."

"We've had a rash of burglaries and purse snatchings here in the past month or so," the officer went on. "I got a good look at your man and have radioed a description down to headquarters."

"My, that was fast!" she remarked with admiration.

"I've got to get back to the traffic, but I've asked for another officer to come and take a statement from you. Wait here."

At that moment, Edward Bartlett reached Germaine. He was clearly shaken.

"Germaine, child, are you alright?" he asked with great concern.

"Oh Edward, I'm fine. I'm sorry I left you there like that, I guess my adrenaline just kicked in. You weren't hurt were you?" she asked her old friend.

"It wasn't me he pushed! I'm so glad you aren't hurt."

"I'm not hurt, but I'll be much happier when I find that locket!"

"Is it gone?" he gasped.

And as Edward looked on, Germaine felt about in her bag. At last, her face relaxed into a smile as her fingers found the brocade bag she had fashioned for the locket the previous day.

"I have it, Edward." She said with clear relief.

"Nothing taken then, miss?" asked a second police officer who had come to take her statement. "Your wallet's intact?"

"Oh, my wallet. Hold on, please," Germaine asked politely as she shuffled through the contents. "Yes, officer, everything is here. Nothing has been taken."

Germaine recounted the story of the purse snatching from her perspective, and Edward Bartlett added his description of the fellow. Edward wondered if the man might have followed them from his jewelry store. The police officer promised to send additional patrols to the street where Edward's and other antique and jewelry shops were located.

"Officer O'Reilly got a good look at the culprit, and that plus your detailed descriptions should lead us to him in no time," said Officer Walsh.

Finally, Germaine and Edward were allowed to go on their way, and they traced their steps back to the restaurant. The paper placemats in the restaurant featured advertisements for the two candidates for the Senate race: Aubrey Bowles, III and

Peter Donaghue, along with information about shoe repair, chimney cleaning, and funeral homes.

"Mr. Donaghue was a good governor," Germaine stated, looking at the faces of the two men staring up from the table in the Mandarin Palace. "I don't know much about Aubrey Bowles, though. Do you?" she asked, remembering all the signs she'd seen on her drive out here.

"As much as I care to," Edward said with a sniff. "His brother Hugo is decent enough, but Aubrey's a bad sort. A man died at the plant, and his wife didn't have any insurance on him. Three young children at home, and no insurance, how was she going to live? Well, it turns out that Aubrey had taken out life insurance policies on the workers in the plant. Nice boss, eh? He got a million dollars from the death of the man, and the widow and children got nothing. The widow went to the Bowles family ready to make a stink and call the newspaper and what have you, but Hugo took care of it. He made Aubrey give the widow the proceeds from the life insurance policy, and it never became public. Hugo's the only decent one in that family."

"How do you know all this Edward?" asked Germaine, sipping her Oolong tea.

"The widow came to me to sell some family heirlooms — a lovely diamond brooch and earrings that were her great grandmother's. She clearly didn't want to sell them, and she told me the story of her husband's death and how they would receive no insurance because of Aubrey Bowles' underhanded deed. I recommended an attorney to her, and she managed to save her jewels and recover the insurance money. She gave me regular updates on the doings, and I have not held Mr. Aubrey Bowles III in very high esteem ever since."

"Why would Aubrey want to be a Senator?" Germaine asked.

"He's a failed businessman. A liar. A cheat and a rogue. Perfect qualities for a politician," said Edward with a wry smile.

Germaine decided to change the subject. "How's your egg foo young?" she asked.

"Perfect. How's *your* egg foo young?" her companion asked.

"Perfect," she smiled, concluding a routine they had shared since childhood when "egg foo young" were the only words Germaine could read on the menu at the Mandarin Palace. Her parents had brought her to visit Edward Bartlett for the day and hearing her sing-song voice say those words made everyone laugh. It instantly became the little group's favorite dish.

As they finished their meals, a waiter at a nearby table dropped a pu-pu platter on the floor, to the great exasperation of the diners who had ordered it.

"There is never a dull moment when you're around, Germaine," Edward joked. "Maybe I should be glad you don't visit me more often!"

Germaine smiled and vowed to make more visits to her aging friend. "Here, Edward," she said, handing him a plate with fortune cookies on it. "Let's see what the future holds…"

Edward opened his and read "Happiness is before you. A true fortune at last! With you across the table, happiness is indeed before me.

"What does yours say, dear?" Edward continued with a smile. Neither diner really believed in fortune telling, but they both enjoyed this traditional ritual at the end of the meal.

"Someone close is deceiving you. Well, that's a bit grim," Germaine remarked.

"Hmmm…. Maybe your chums are planning a big surprise party for you." Edward joked, hoping to brighten the mood, but secretly worrying that the fortune might prove an ominous warning. He didn't like the idea of Germaine carrying around such a valuable object as the locket, but he knew that she wouldn't hear of locking it up while she was researching it.

As they finished up, Germaine noted that it was getting late, and she hoped to get back to Springdale before dark to dig around in the garden a bit more. The pair walked back to Bartlett's Family Jewels, Germaine maintaining a tight grip on her purse, and they both talked happily, yet remained vigilant for thieves on the street.

Chapter Four: One step forward

As Germaine motored over to Elmhurst to meet with Dr. Dupre, she thought over the previous day's purse snatching. Had she been the target of such a rash attempt because the thief had seen the locket? Were Edward's customers in danger? Was Edward in danger? Had the thief seen the locket in Frau Kroch's shop? She tried to remember if anyone else had been in the stationery store, but was unsuccessful. She knew she'd been alone in Edward's jewelry store, but someone could have peered in the window and seen the large gold locket. Perhaps it was just a random crime.

She put all of those thoughts out of her mind as she locked her car and made her way towards the ivy-covered Samuelson Hall of Elmhurst College where Dr. Dupre had his office. The demure heels of Germaine's shoes clicked upon the old bricks underfoot. She looked around and took in centuries of history. The venerable institution was celebrating its bicentennial that year. It was one of the three oldest colleges in the country. While most of the buildings now on campus had been built in the nineteenth century, there were a few from the eighteenth century, when the school was founded as an institution to educate ministers in the new lands of America. It had grown considerably since then and now offered liberal arts and science courses, as well as being a place to educate ministers.

Germaine pushed open the heavy walnut entry doors to Samuelson Hall. She made her way up the worn marble stairs and easily found room 207. Dr. Emile Dupre arose from behind a heavily carved Jacobean library table that served as his desk. The bookshelves that lined every wall of the small office were filled with books, academic journals, students' papers, and photographs.

"Germaine, my dear! It's been far too long!" Emile Dupre said, as he embraced Germaine warmly.

A young woman was seated with her back to Germaine. She rose with a tight smile and held out her hand limply. "I've heard so much about you. I'm Claudia Saunders."

"Claudia is my most promising student since you were here at Elmhurst, Germaine," Dr. Emile Dupre said with a warm smile. "She is no-nonsense, all about the facts. A first-rate researcher!"

"It's a pleasure to meet you Miss Saunders," Germaine said, shaking the young woman's disappointingly listless hand.

"Likewise," Claudia muttered drily.

"Well let's see what you have Germaine! I've been curious about it ever since you called. Claudia, make sure you take good notes," Dr. Dupre instructed.

Germaine drew the brocade velvet pouch she had made out of her handbag. She thought of how close the locket had come to being stolen or run over by a car, and she shuddered.

"Are you cold, Germaine?" Dr. Dupre asked solicitously.

"No, no. I'm fine," Germaine said. "Here it is." And with that, she laid the locket out on her former professor's desk. He admired the case for a moment and then asked her to open it.

"The ornament is lovely, but the real treasure is these photos!" he said with excitement as he examined the photographs under a magnifying glass.

"Victorian... silver process... considerable foxing...," he described all the physical attributes of the photographs as Claudia Saunders diligently wrote down his thoughts. "The background appears identical... taken in a studio... Springdale or Boston... ah ha!" he exclaimed suddenly, "I'd say these portraits were made in the mid-1870s, and I do believe we will soon know where."

The young women looked at each other wondering how Dr. Dupre would identify the location of the photographs, as he gently pried each one from the locket, using a special implement that greatly resembled ordinary tweezers. "See that?" he asked rather triumphantly.

Neither girl could see anything particular about the photos, so they both leaned in and nearly bumped heads.

"Germaine, take the magnifying glass," he said, passing the glass to her. "In the lower right-hand corner. What do you see?"

"Oh! It's quite clear with the magnifier!" Germaine said, as Claudia Saunders awaited her turn impatiently.

"What is it?" Dr. Dupre's student said after Germaine passed her the magnifying glass. "I don't see anything."

"Germaine," the professor said, "show her what she's missing."

Germaine pointed to a small painted design in the lower right hand corner of the portrait. On first glance, it appeared to form part of the patterned background in the photographer's studio, but upon closer examination it proved to be a signature of a sort. It was the stylized AMG of the A.M. Giroux photographic studio, a prolific firm that went into business in Springdale at the conclusion of the Civil War. The studio changed its AMG symbol each year, and Dr. Dupre's years of expertise made it immediately apparent to him that what he was looking at was the 1872 mark.

"Oh," Claudia said, hastily writing down some notations.

"Okay," Germaine said. "1872, from Springdale, A. M. Giroux studios, possibly taken the same day. Now we just need to know who they are, and why two American portraits from 1872 were in a locket that has an 1885 French hallmark!"

Germaine decided that Dr. Dupre wouldn't be especially interested in the key and the hidden compartment, so she didn't mention them.

"That's where Claudia comes in. She is a fine researcher, and if you'll agree, I'd like to have her investigate who these young ladies might be."

Germaine was happy to agree to this arrangement. She esteemed Dr. Dupre immensely and was sure that anyone he recommended for the job would do a thorough job of investigating.

"Let's just take this other photo out, and we'll make copies of them so that you can take the originals home with you," Dr. Dupre said, removing the portrait on the right. "Oh ho! What have we here?" he exclaimed as a tiny pressed maple leaf fluttered on to his desk.

Germaine told Dr. Dupre and his student assistant that she had found the locket buried in her garden under a clump of flowers. "It's probably just from being underground," Claudia said.

"I don't think so," Germaine said gently. "This is a pressed leaf," she said, holding it up to show Miss Saunders. "And this locket has a very tight closure. If the leaf got in from being buried, there would be dirt inside the locket."

"Quite right, Germaine. Miss Saunders is good, but she has some catching up to do to reach you!" said the goodnatured professor. Germaine noticed that this comment upset her professor's assistant.

"Oh, I only know this from working with you when I was a student. I'm quite sure Miss Saunders is already an excellent researcher and will only improve with more practice," she said with a smile, hoping to put the other young woman at ease.

"Quite so!" Dr. Dupre agreed.

Claudia Saunders looked down at her notepad and said nothing, embarrassed both by Germaine's praise and by her shortcoming being pointed out.

"Well, Claudia," Dr. Dupre said, "What say you find out who this belonged to?"

"Yes, sir," she said quietly. Germaine gave Claudia her address and sketched out a plan of the garden, indicating where she found the locket.

"Perhaps they were French Canadians like the Moreaus and the Dupres," chuckled Dr. Dupre, "and that's why there's a maple leaf inside."

"You might be right," Germaine replied, "There were many French Canadians in Springdale, and throughout New England, even before the Civil War. And the maple leaf has been a symbol of Canada for quite some time."

"Claudia," Dr. Dupre turned to address his young assistant, "Do you have all the information you need to get started?"

"Yes, sir," she responded without hesitation.

"Very well then, let's see what you can dig up about these photos." She nodded and gathered up her things, then shook Germaine's hand mumbling something that Germaine took to be some sort of pleasantry, and she made her way out of the room.

"I dare say," said Dr. Dupre, straightening some papers on his carved desk, "we here at Elmhurst are still waiting for the day when we have a class of students as strong as yours, Germaine. You, Helen Potter, Chauncey Fetterson, William Deveraux, Charles Morgan, Catherine Fielding…" he trailed off wistfully. "And you're all doing fine things with the education you got here at the college."

"I shall be seeing Helen quite soon, Dr. Dupre," Germaine said. Helen Potter, Germaine Moreau and Chauncey Fetterson had been the top three students in their class, and had a friendly rivalry to get the best grades. The three developed a lasting friendship, and all settled in Springdale after college. Helen worked as a curator at the Springdale Historical Museum. One of her areas of expertise was cryptology, and she had correspondents throughout the world who sent coded messages to her to crack. Chauncey Fetterson became an architect who specialized in historic preservation and renovation. "Helen and I are in touch a great deal, but we haven't heard from Chauncey in a while. He's been busy with the Symphony Hall project,"

Germaine said, referencing a prestigious historical commission their friend had won.

"Yes, yes, I remember reading about that in the *Gazette*," their former professor said. "If and when you see either or both, please send my regards," he concluded with a courtly flourish.

"Indeed I will," Germaine curtsied facetiously in return.

Germaine returned home in the early evening and found a note from Mrs. White, her housekeeper, on the kitchen table. The note said that there was a nice dinner in the fridge. The only telephone message Germaine had received while she was out had been from Federicka Kroch who had telephoned to thank her for the flowers. Germaine looked through the day's mail and, seeing nothing of immediate importance, decided to follow a hunch. She changed into her gardening clothes, which Mrs. White had laundered and pressed, and began digging under the large maple tree that stood in one corner of the garden.

"Maybe the box is buried under this maple tree," she thought as she plunged her shovel into the dirt, hoping to hear the noise of her shovel hitting metal. She dug holes and probed with the shovel handle, but didn't find a thing except rocks and roots. After about an hour, she put the shovel down and looked around. The garden was a terrible mess. There were holes and piles of dirt all around the maple tree, and the other plants were tangled and brown.

Germaine sighed. Not one to give up easily, she decided that she was more interested in discovering who the rightful owner of the locket was than she was in getting her garden together. She estimated it might take a few weeks of research to find out to whom the locket belonged, and possibly months before she could track those people down, even if they hadn't moved out of the Springdale area. Realizing that she would also be working on decorating jobs from around the world, she decided to hire someone to work in the garden.

Germaine remembered that Mrs. McGrath, a long-time neighbor, had told her that her grandson Andrew would be spending the summer in Springdale before he went off to the state college in the nearby town of Glenfield. Andrew was a hardy young man, and Mr. McGrath didn't want him to be idle all summer, so the grandparents had let all the neighbors know that they could call on him for odd jobs around the house.

There were only a few couples of Mr. and Mrs. McGrath's generation still in the neighborhood. Some had moved south to escape the cold New England winters, while still others had moved in with their grown children when they couldn't manage the stairs and general upkeep of their homes. Germaine admired the McGraths' stamina in keeping up their big old house, but she wanted to make sure that if she asked Andrew McGrath to help her in the garden, she wouldn't be taking him away from helping those older folks who needed the help more than she did.

She sat down at the telephone table in the downstairs hallway to dial the McGraths' number. It was Mr. McGrath who answered. Germaine explained her predicament and the man seemed thrilled to have a job for his grandson that required physical labor.

"That's capital, Germaine! The boy needs some real work to keep him out of trouble," he chuckled. "We old timers just ask him to change a light bulb or some such nonsense, but digging up that old garden is the kind of labor that eighteen year

old boys are meant to do. When do you want him to start?"

Chapter Five: Two steps back

As soon as Germaine awoke the next morning, she reviewed the previous few days' events: the drive to Chalmsford, Edward Bartlett's valuation of her locket, Frau Kroch's unscrambling of the monogram, the purse snatching, the fortune cookie, her visit to Dr. Dupre, the pressed maple leaf hidden behind one of the photos... There was much to consider.

What lock did the key open? That question was uppermost in Germaine's mind as she made her way to the kitchen. But as soon as she saw the kitchen in a slight state of disarray she realized she hadn't tidied up before she went to bed, which was most unlike her. She was glad she would have someone else to do the gardening so she wouldn't let other things pile up. Mrs. White didn't come until late morning, so Germaine had plenty of time to clean up before the housekeeper arrived. She made her breakfast first, and read the morning paper. She wanted to make sure she mailed a thank you note to Dr. Dupre and Claudia Saunders before the postman came at noon, so after she tidied up the kitchen and washed up her breakfast things, she sat down at the little writing desk in the parlor and penned gracious and personal notes to them both.

Andrew McGrath arrived promptly at nine o'clock, which Germaine took as a very good indicator of his character. Germaine wanted to chat with the youngster before letting him have free reign in the garden. She needed to make sure that he knew how important it was to follow Miss Rose's plan and not change anything from the original plot. She also wanted to feel that she could trust him to tell her if he happened to find a priceless Russian chest of jewels buried in her Springdale garden.

"My goodness, Andrew," Germaine exclaimed upon seeing the McGrath youth, "you're all grown up! The last time I saw you, you were about four feet tall!"

"Hello, Miss Germaine. I'm so glad I can help you while I'm staying with my grandmother and grandfather," the boy said. "What do you want to do with the garden? It's kind of a mess back here."

Germaine explained the request from Miss Rose not to make any changes to the garden, and she showed him the original garden plan and photographs. "Do you think you can handle this?" she asked.

"Well, it will definitely keep me busy," said the youth. "When do you want it done?"

"It will take as long as it takes; I would say at least a few weeks, don't you think so?" she asked, and the boy nodded in agreement.

"Let's do this, Andrew. You start in the north corner. That's where the vegetables need to go, and I want to start growing them as soon as possible so I have a good crop. Also, the things with roots there should just be weeds, so that shouldn't take very long. You know that I am an historian, right Andrew?"

He nodded.

"As such, I am very interested in any objects found in the garden. You know, old rakes or garden implements, pottery shards, arrowheads, that kind of thing."

Again, Andrew nodded.

"I want to be very clear that if you find any non-plant or rock material that you will tell me immediately and don't throw anything away. Is it a deal?"

"Deal," said Andrew McGrath. "I can start today, if that's okay with you."

"That's perfect," said Germaine, impressed that the quiet youth was ready to get started.

And with that Germaine went inside, relieved to have taken the task of gardening off of her very full list of things to do.

After she neatly tucked away the understatedly elegant stationery that she had used to write her thank you notes, Germaine scanned the home for possible hiding places that could hold a precious Russian box. She was sure she knew every nook and cranny of the old Sheppard home. As a result of the scavenger hunts her parents had devised for her when she was a child, she had discovered hidden compartments in two of the home's four fireplaces, and a hidden room in the attic. The secret compartments in the fireplaces were empty, but the hidden room in the attic contained lots of old papers: letters and journals mostly, plus old bills and household paperwork. She had been too young to care about them when she had first found the room. As a girl, she couldn't really make out the difficult old-fashioned handwriting, and she hadn't really thought about the room or its contents in all these years. Germaine made a mental note to re-explore the fireplaces later, but first decided to head up to the attic to examine the hidden room.

She kept a flashlight hanging on the inside doorknob to the attic. She turned it on and used the weak beam to get her bearings in the attic. She had to move several boxes of Christmas ornaments, Halloween decorations, old art projects she had created as a child, and a collection of antique lamps that needed to be re-wired, but she finally reached her destination: a wooden wall that looked just like all the other walls in the old attic, except that it was ever so slightly bowed in one corner. The childlike thrill of discovery came flooding back to her. "There was a button on the floor," she remembered, "under this scrap of linoleum..." and as she said these words, her foot depressed the button and the false wall swung open. "Ah ha!" she said with glee, and hurried into the little room. The flashlight's beam was dim, but was enough to illuminate the contents of the hide-a-way. It was just as she'd remembered it. Small boxes neatly stacked in two rows on the floor in one corner, and a solid old bookcase along the other wall.

As she beamed her light along the bookcase, she saw that it was filled with rows and rows of small, leather-bound notebooks. "That's right!" Germaine exclaimed, "Miss Rose's diaries." Germaine recalled that Miss Rose had been a dedicated chronicler of the events of her life and the world around her. Until her final days, she had made daily entries of the things that mattered to her. And here they all were – a life and a history lesson right over Germaine's head all this time. When she had first discovered them, Miss Rose's diaries held no significance. But during her years at college, Germaine had come to appreciate the importance of ordinary people's recollections. In fact, Germaine had taken a class called "First Hand, Third Hand" which compared historical figures' and ordinary people's recollections of important historical events with what was reported in the newspapers. "How could I have forgotten this treasure?" she wondered. "Oh well. What's important is that I've remembered it now," she said with determination, picking up one of the volumes.

Miss Rose had meticulously dated each one, and Germaine decided to start at the beginning, when Rose Santini was eighteen years old. Germaine took the first five volumes, which covered Miss Rose's life from eighteen to twenty-five and carefully made sure the others didn't get jumbled up. She pushed all the holiday decorations and other things back against another wall so that it would be easier to access this nook in the future, and made her way downstairs. Germaine's library was across the hall from her bedroom. She put the journals down on the library desk, and popped into the bedroom to make sure it would pass Mrs. White's muster later that day. When she was satisfied her bedroom was tidy enough, she crossed the hall into the library, took out a pair of white cotton conservator's gloves so she wouldn't mar any of the ink or stain the delicate old paper, and sat down with the journals.

She read through page after page of discussions about family, servants, world events, New England events, Springdale society, neighborhood doings, and the weather. It was interesting stuff indeed, but did nothing to explain the locket, the initials LSS, the golden key, the word *"evermore"*, or the dried maple leaf. As Germaine was reading, she heard the back door open and shut and knew Mrs. White had arrived. She called down a greeting to the faithful housekeeper, and it was returned happily. Mrs. White was a bit like a grandmother to Germaine; she had been with the family since Germaine was a child, and often babysat for young Germaine when her parents were out gallivanting around the world.

Mrs. White always made lunch for the two of them as well as whatever guests might be there, and today was no exception. A few hours after her arrival, she called up to Germaine that lunch was ready, and Germaine came bounding down the stairs with a journal in hand.

"Oh Mrs. White," Germaine beamed, giving the housekeeper a warm peck on the cheek, "you'll never believe everything that's happened since last week!"

"What sort of an adventure have you gotten involved in this time," asked the skeptical older woman.

"A historical one!" her young friend exclaimed.

"Well, nothing that can't wait until you've eaten some tomato soup and grilled cheese sandwiches," said Mrs. White, setting the table.

And with that, they sat down to a homey lunch during which Germaine caught Mrs. White up on the discovery of the diaries.

"Heavens to Murgatroid!" said the housekeeper. "That is quite a story. I wonder who those people are?" she asked, as she peered at the photos in the locket.

"And you haven't heard the latest clue," said Germaine with a smile. "This entry is from when Miss Rose was in her forties: 'Today I learned a somber story about the family and the jewels. I don't even dare to write it in my diary. But I will <u>forget it not</u>. '" She read the underlined diary entry dramatically, and paused to await Mrs. White's reaction.

"Do you think it has to do with the forget-me-nots?" asked the housekeeper.

"Indeed I do!" Germaine said with satisfaction. "The locket was buried under a mound of forget-me-nots."

"Well, that certainly does seem symbolic. But what on earth does that key go to? You know every corner of this house. Have you ever seen a little lock that would take a tiny key like that?"

"No. And that makes it even more mysterious," said Germaine. "I must figure out what the key unlocks and who the Sheppards' rightful heirs are."

"Well, if you can't find them, I'll make a sacrifice and take the locket off your hands. I'm sure I can find someone in my family tree with the initials LSS," Mrs. White said with a wink.

"You'll have to get in line after Edward Bartlett," Germaine replied, happily joking with her trusted housekeeper, while silently wondering if there were indeed more secret hiding places in the old Sheppard house that she didn't know about.

Her thoughts were interrupted by the ringing of the telephone. Mrs. White announced it was a Miss Claudia Saunders on the line.

"I'm impressed," Germaine said to the other girl, "I didn't think you'd have any answers this quickly."

"I spent the whole day researching your photos," Claudia Saunders said drily. "I am almost one hundred percent sure that the women are a mother and daughter who lived in Springdale until the Civil War. They were both nurses and went to the front to help the troops. Their names were Harriet and Margaret Stevens. Harriet was the mother. Her husband died of typhoid just before the Civil War started. The women felt bad that they hadn't been able to save him, and dedicated their lives to saving others. They owned the land that your house was built on. In fact, they owned all the land that later became Beaumont Street. They sold it all to G. Taylor Wood, who built it up during the war."

"That's very interesting," Germaine interrupted, "but the locket was made in 1885 and Dr. Dupre says the photographs are from 1872. The Sheppard house was built in 1867 – how and why would the Stevenses have buried a locket with photographs of themselves in someone else's back garden?"

"I just assume that they missed their old land and decided to put something there as a memento. According to the land survey G. Taylor Wood conducted just before building the houses on the street, there was a very large, very old maple tree right around the spot where you found the locket, but it was taken down when the land was developed," said Claudia icily.

"So you think they were sentimental ladies and plucked a leaf of a maple tree, and buried the locket where their old maple tree had been?" Germaine asked.

"It stands to reason," Claudia replied.

"And what about the initials on the locket, LSS?" Germaine asked, failing to see a connection.

"Harriet's husband and Margaret's father was Lewis Stanley Stevens," Claudia responded, offering what she thought was conclusive proof that the locket was theirs.

Since Germaine hadn't mentioned the key to Dr. Dupre or Claudia Saunders when she saw them, she didn't feel she should mention it now. Still, Claudia's explanation didn't sit right with Germaine.

"Where did the Stevens women go after the war?" Germaine asked, trying to understand what would have brought them to the Sheppards' back garden to bury a precious piece of jewelry with their photos inside.

"Ah... um..." Claudia Saunders hesitated, and Germaine was sure she was going to say she didn't know, but then Claudia surprised Germaine by saying, "They went to Canada, just as you and Dr. Dupre speculated. I was just looking for it in my notes," she said in a rushed tone. Germaine heard some papers rustling over the telephone.

"Hmmm," Germaine said, non-committally. "We were half-joking about Canada because of the maple leaf. What a strange coincidence... Where in Canada did they go, Claudia? Is that in your notes?"

Claudia rustled some more papers. "Toronto," she said in her usual clipped voice.

"Well, thank you, Miss Saunders, for your quick and thorough work," Germaine said, appreciating Claudia's effort. "Did you happen to find any heirs of the Stevens women, either in Toronto or here in the states? I should like to return the locket to them if it is theirs. I'm sure they'd like the photos of their relatives very much."

"They both died childless. No heirs," Claudia said quickly.

"Well, Harriet didn't exactly die childless if Margaret was her daughter," Germaine said gently.

"I mean childless after that. No heirs. Case closed."

"Okay... Well, thank you again, Miss Saunders. I appreciate your help in this matter," Germaine said, disappointed that she seemed to have reached a dead end in finding out to whom the locket rightfully belonged, and what the elaborate key might open.

Germaine wondered if the Springdale Historical Museum might have some records of the Stevens family in its archives. She thought that there were perhaps other branches of the family listed that she could reach out to regarding the locket and photos. "Why would the Stevens women have come all the way down here from Toronto just to bury a locket with such old photos? They must have been near the ends of their lives in 1885. Maybe they wanted to leave some sort of legacy. Perhaps that is what '*evermore*' meant," Germaine mulled these thoughts over and over. As she went outside to check on Andrew

McGrath's progress in the garden, she decided to put the Stevens family out of her mind until she went to the museum the next day.

"You are doing a fine job, Andrew," Germaine said approvingly as she surveyed the work that Andrew had completed in the garden.

"Thanks, Miss Germaine," he replied, pleased with the praise. "I've found a couple of strange things so far, and put them all near the shed for you, like you asked."

Germaine's heart skipped a beat. Had one of those strange things been the ornate Russian chest that would be unlocked by the key in the locket?

"It's mostly old pieces of broken pottery, but I did find one neat thing – a little box," said Andrew, walking beside Germaine to the shed.

"Let's see," Germaine said, trying to sound as calm as possible as her heart raced with the thought that it might contain the mate to the tiny key.

Chapter Six: A lie discovered

Andrew pointed to a small dirt-covered box. "There it is," he said.

"Oh!" Germaine exclaimed with surprise. "That's a snuff box. And it's an old one. I would say it's from before the American Revolution," Germaine's interest in this surprising discovery nearly compensated for her disappointment that it wasn't the jewel chest that had been unearthed.

"Snuff boxes were used to hold sniffing tobacco and they became an essential possession for gentleman ever since the days when Europeans first discovered tobacco here in the colonies," she said, as she brushed the dirt off the silver. "I'll take this inside and clean it up properly," she said. "And tomorrow I'll show you what it looks like without all the dirt." Germaine and Andrew picked through the other odds and ends he'd found in the garden, but there was nothing else of great historical interest, and certainly no exquisite golden box.

"I'll be sure to tell your grandfather what a fine job you're doing," she said as she bade the young McGrath boy good night.

The next morning, Germaine cleaned off the snuff box and discovered that it was engraved with a coat of arms. The hallmarks on the bottom of the box were English, and Germaine concluded that it had belonged to an early Springdale settler.

She brought the snuff box up to her library and found a reference book on heraldry. After leafing through a few chapters, she found that the divided chevron, falcon and lion rampant were the crest of a specific branch of the Stevens family of Kent. Germaine sighed, "This makes what Claudia said even more likely to be true. I hope I can find their heirs at the library today."

She brought the cleaned up snuff box and book on heraldry downstairs. She thought Andrew might be interested in learning what she'd found about the object when he arrived.

"Why is it called a lion rampant?" he asked, intrigued by the symbolism of the coat of arms. Germaine explained that the term simply referred to an animal standing on its left hind leg, and that a lion standing in such a manner was a symbol of strength and valor.

"And what about the falcon?" he asked, intrigued.

"The falcon is a symbol of speed and strength," Germaine replied. "All heraldic crests or coats of arms are designed to make the family look powerful, but even the little triangles and stripes have special names and meanings. I still have more research to do to identify precisely to whom this little box might have belonged, and when it was made."

"How did you learn all of that?" Andrew asked, in awe.

"I probably started learning these things when I was about your age," Germaine replied. "My parents were both historians, so we had a lot of books around the house. In fact, this book on heraldry was my father's," she said, patting the large reference book.

"But I also spent a lot of time at the library and at the Historical Society. They offer lots of classes to the public about history. I'm going there today, would you like me to pick up a schedule for you?"

Andrew said he would like that very much, and went off to work in the garden, as interested in finding more old objects as he was in getting the garden itself cleaned up and planted.

Germaine sat down at the little writing desk in the downstairs hallway to make a list of the things she wanted to research at the Historical Society: A.M. Giroux photography studio, the Stevens family history in Springdale, G. Taylor Wood's development of Beaumont Street, and the Stevens family coat of arms.

Germaine sat for a moment and admired the delicate marquetry along the edge of the little writing desk. She remembered the time she had spent with her parents in the Marche region of Italy, where marquetry was most refined and whence it got its name, and the moment she had seen this desk in an antique shop in the foothills of Urbino. Its small scale was just right for a girl of fourteen, and her parents were so impressed with her taste that they bought it for her and had it shipped back to Springdale.

She was jolted out of her reverie by the ring of the telephone. Rodney Bennett, the retired president of a company that made motorized golf carts, was on the line. Mr. Bennett had developed a passion for Colonial furniture and design, and had purchased an early American home in Vermont that was about to be demolished. He was rebuilding it board by board in Springdale. He wanted to know if Germaine could find a source for reproduction early American floorcloths.

"I think a checkerboard pattern would work, but I want it to be authentic to the period," he said. Nothing that came into production after 1780. Do you think you can help?"

"Certainly, Mr. Bennett. In fact, I am on my way to the Springdale Historical Museum this morning, and I should be able to find an answer for you today," said Germaine, much to Mr. Bennett's pleasure.

She added Rodney Bennett's request to her list and headed out the door. When she arrived, she picked up a schedule of classes and lectures that the society would be offering for Andrew. Helen Potter greeted her longtime friend warmly. "Oh Germaine, how good it is to see you! This fine weather is bringing everyone outside," she said with a smile. "Chauncey just left."

"Oh, I am sorry I missed him," Germaine said honestly. "Is he still working on the Symphony Hall renovation?" Chauncey Fetterson had won a highly competitive commission to renovate the beautiful Springdale Symphony Hall and was nearing the end of the two-year project. He had been so busy with that work that the other two friends had not seen him as frequently as they liked.

"Frankly," Helen admitted, "I don't know what he was up to. He barely said hello and just marched straight into the archives room.

"I was busy doing research for a professor at the State University. I figured if he needed help, he'd be the first to ask," she said with a smile as she and Germaine both silently considered the somewhat bossy nature of their college chum.

"Well I do need help!" Germaine exclaimed. "I have a list. First off, I need to find out about early American floorcloths for Rodney Bennett. What designs were in production during this period, and who currently manufactures reproduction versions?"

"Easy enough," said Helen, thinking of the annually updated Colonial Resources catalog the Society kept in the reference section.

"Next, is there a list of the different marks that the A.M. Giroux photography studio used by year?"

"Indeed there is," Helen answered.

"Great. I don't suppose there's a list of sitters by date," Germaine said wistfully.

"Wouldn't that be nice!" Helen said laughing. "You might be surprised to learn how many people come here looking to find out who a person is in a photograph with no background information at all."

"Add me to that list," Germaine said. "I have two photographs, one key, one golden locket, a pressed maple leaf, and a silver snuff box that I'm trying to identify. And I have very little to go on!" Germaine told her good friend and fellow historian about everything she had discovered in the garden, her visits to Chalmsford and Elmhurst, and the old diaries of Miss Rose Santini.

"Good grief, Germaine!" Helen said when she had heard the whole tale. "Let's get started! I'll take care of Mr. Bennett's research, and you head into the archives. I'll meet you back there as soon as I find out about the floorcloth, and I'll bring the A.M. Giroux records."

"By the way," Germaine added, "Dr. Dupre sends his regards."

Helen was very happy to hear that their former professor was part of this research project.

Germaine situated herself at a long, empty table in the archive room. From her briefcase, she withdrew a notebook and several pencils, and placed these on the table in front of her. There were a few other amateur historians at other tables and carrels in the records room. People came from all over to do genealogical research on Springdale relations, and after suffering an attempted purse snatching in Chalmsford, she thought she had best keep her briefcase in arm's reach.

Germaine walked purposefully up and down the aisles, pulling things from the shelves. When she could carry no more, she returned to the table where she had placed her note-taking equipment and deposited the stacks of research material on the old wooden table. "How many people have sat here over the years?" she asked herself as she admired the rich patina of the aged wood.

"I wonder if Miss Rose herself ever sat right here where I'm sitting?" she continued in her imagination. The Springdale Historical Museum had been built during the Great Depression, and Germaine knew that Miss Rose had been one of the people in the community who had donated large sums of money during that difficult time to build the museum and establish its collections. The important families of Springdale had wanted to make sure that their collective history was not lost, and they hoped to do something to provide work for the many people who had lost their jobs as factories closed around the region. It had been so well-designed and well-built that no structural or decorative changes had been required in all these years. The shelves, the tables, the chairs, the desks, and the storage units were all the ones installed originally. Germaine had always admired the pride of craftsmanship taken by the workers and the foresight of the designers who had created this important building, and aimed for a similar timelessness in her own designs.

She turned to the stack of material before her. She had found city directories, rolls of microfilm, boxes of clippings, and personal scrapbooks related to the Stevens family, G. Taylor Wood, Beaumont Street and the Sheppard house that Germaine now occupied. She decided to start with the city directories. The first one that she took from the shelf was from 1882. Telephones were not widely in use yet, and the directory was arranged in alphabetical order by street, rather than by last name, and then in numeric order. People's professions were also listed by abbreviation, but there was no key to these abbreviations, and they were not standardized at all. One fisherman might be listed as "Henry Fields, fsm," while his neighbor Gus Parker might have been a "fsh." Germaine slipped on a pair of clean cotton conservator's gloves, and carefully turned to the first of the "B" pages. She found Beaumont Street quickly and scanned through the street numbers. "1, 3, 5, 7, 9..... It only goes up to 25 Beaumont Street. I guess that part of the street hadn't been developed with houses yet," thought Germaine, putting the directory to the side. "Perhaps the Stevenses sold the land as separate parcels over the years," she offered.

Germaine looked over some of the historical and biographical information about the Stevenses, and learned that they had arrived in Springdale during the second wave of English settlement, in the 1690s. Springdale was first settled in 1601 by five English families, the Chapin, Rice, Richardson, Taylor, and Fletcher families. They created roads, and built homes and a church. They also built a wall to protect the tiny settlement against the French and the Indians, and the same structure was eventually used for protection from their English countrymen. The small group that first arrived in Springdale was so successful with the corn, tobacco, and wheat they grew and shipped back to England that more families followed. The Stevens family was among these. They had been a wealthy family in Shropshire, but had fallen on hard times and multiple female births. The family's only son, John, decided to strike out on his own in the colonies and see if he could regain the family's fortune.

According to the papers in the Historical Society's archives, Jacob Stevens claimed a large swath of land overlooking the river when he arrived. He farmed it successfully and sent lots of money back home to Shropshire. He settled in Springdale and the family continued for several generations, even though each generation typically only produced one son and several daughters. Lewis Stanley Stevens appears to have been the final male of the Stevens line. "Harriet and Margaret left the United States after the Civil War, heartbroken about the rift between countrymen," Germaine read in a news article that had been published in 1901 to celebrate the tercentennial of Springdale's founding, "and moved to Toronto, Canada, where they both died, never again setting foot in their homeland."

"How can that be?" Germaine said out loud, putting down the newspaper article and scratching her head.

"How can what be?" Helen Potter asked her friend as she sat down beside her. The other researchers had left and the two girls were now alone in the large room.

"How can Harriet and Margaret Stevens have never returned to the United States and also have had their photos taken at the A.M. Giroux studio in 1872?"

"I don't know," said Helen. "But here are the Giroux studio's marks by year, and a write-up about how they were famous for their system of changing their studio mark by year. Perhaps a Canadian photography studio copied them?"

"Perhaps…" Germaine said, her voice trailing off as she looked at the studio's clever dating system.

"Helen, would you pass me those street directories please?" Germaine asked. Her friend complied, and the two girls looked over the residents listed by house number in 1865, 1866, and 1867. There were more and more homes built each year, but there was nothing listed at 32 Beaumont until the 1867 edition.

"Beaumont, 32, Mr. Lyman Sheppard, mrch. & faml.," the two read in unison.

"But that's before Claudia said the land was sold," Helen said, surprised.

"It is indeed," Germaine said, having already understood that some aspects of Claudia Saunders' story did not really add up. "Let's see that topographical report for 1866," she went on.

Helen unrolled the survey on the table, and Germaine gave a wry grin. "Just as I thought," she whispered. "There is no maple tree there," she said as she pointed to the spot on the map that corresponded to the place where she found the locket, "and it clearly states that G. Taylor Wood is the owner of all that land." Her voice rose as she said this last part.

"Why would Claudia Saunders lie?" Helen asked with concern.

Chapter Seven: Treasure hunting

"Lie is a strong word. Let's not jump to any conclusions," Germaine replied. "All her other research so far checks out."

"Germaine, you always see the good in everyone. It can be quite frustrating!" Helen said, smiling.

"Perhaps Claudia jumped to a logical conclusion without completing all the necessary research. I want to give her the benefit of the doubt," Germaine said kindly. "Dr. Dupre said she was one of his best students, but she is still a student. Maybe she just got tired of looking through all the old records and created a convincing story.

"Regardless of what was on Claudia Saunders' mind, what's on my mind is finding out once and for all who those people are in the photos!" Germaine said.

"Pass the 1868 directory, would you Helen?" she asked her friend.

The housing boom that began during the Civil War continued in Springdale right up until the Dull Times, as the national depression of the 1870's was known. Because of Springdale's unique geography, an arsenal had been built on the hill at the top of the city right after America gained its independence. Weapons made in the arsenal were transported along the Connecticut River and over the crisscrossing railroad lines throughout the country. When the Civil War broke out, the demand for arms of all sorts increased dramatically and Springdale underwent a housing boom. The renowned architectural firm of G. Taylor Wood & Co. had been engaged to turn much of the farmland below the Springdale Arsenal into housing for the engineers, gunsmiths, and factory workers who were turning out weapons at a mighty clip during that sad chapter of history.

G. Taylor Wood was a New York based architect who had a complete and clear vision of how the ideal neighborhood should be planned. He drew on the work of Chicago architect and city planner D.H. Burnham to create a plan for an urban neighborhood that would offer residents the perfect mix of public and private space and would be the ideal distance from church and commerce. G. Taylor Wood planned this ideal neighborhood down to the tiniest detail.

"Listen to this," Helen said, reading aloud from the Springdale *Gazette,* "Today, G. Taylor Wood has completed the ninety-ninth, and final, home in Taylor Woods, the ideal neighborhood his firm constructed on the old Stevens farmland below the Arsenal. Springdale is the first community in the United States to have an 'ideal neighborhood' and we are sure many mayors will visit Springdale to learn how it was done, in hopes of replicating this exceptional planned neighborhood. The elegance and good function of Taylor Woods is obvious, and many of Springdale's best families are moving into this fine area."

"I agree that the elegance and good function are indeed obvious," Germaine said, "and as a resident of the neighborhood, I can attest to their durability!"

"'In an interview, Wood said that he built ninety-nine rather than one hundred homes because ninety-nine is a more auspicious number. Wood's precision and planning extends to the interiors of the homes, as well, and each house comes with a suggested plan for decoration. Colors, fabrics, furniture arrangement are all considered by the architect'," Helen read. "That's odd," she said, interrupting her recitation of the old news article. "Why would he want to have a say in people's furnishings?"

"I suppose he imagined his ideal neighborhood down to the smallest detail and wanted the people who would live there to share his vision," Germaine answered. "Do you think he would be pleased with the way the houses look today?"

"I don't know about the others," Helen replied, "but yours is a masterpiece. I'm sure he'd approve."

Germaine smiled and put the street directories and newspaper clippings aside. She turned to the canisters of microfilm that she'd brought to the table. One contained the blueprints and architectural renderings of all the homes in the planned neighborhood of G. Taylor Wood & Co. Germaine looked around for a machine, and brought the roll of microfilm with her. She quickly turned the spool until she found the plans for the houses on Beaumont Street. She paused at number 32 and zoomed in on the details. It was apparent to her that the little secret room in the attic where she had found Miss Rose's diaries was not an original feature of the home. The rest of the very familiar home looked the same, but as she rotated the plans, she noticed a tiny asterisk in the margin of one of the drawings. As she scrolled down the page, she noticed two more of these minute notations. Scanning across the document, she realized that two of the stars were aligned with the two fireplace mantles where she had discovered hidden compartments as a child. The third star corresponded to a space in the basement beside the ash pit that collected all the coal remnants in the days of coal burning heating stoves.

"There's a third secret compartment in the house!" Germaine thought to herself, quietly hoping that the box that matched the key in the locket might be in that basement compartment.

"Helen," Germaine asked with a mischievous grin, "would you like to come on a treasure hunt?"

"That depends on how much digging is involved," Helen replied.

"None. Come and have lunch with me. I think I know where the golden box is to be found. And there is no dirt involved, unless old coal dust counts."

"How could I pass up an offer like that?" Helen smiled. "It's almost one o'clock now. I'll be done with work for the day as soon as Mary O'Leary arrives. She's due at one and she's never late. Let's put all of this stuff back and by the time we're done Mary should be here. Then we can head over to Beaumont Street."

The two friends returned the books to their rightful places on the shelves, re-spooled their microfilm, and straightened the chairs. Soon, they were on their way to Beaumont Street and the Sheppard House. Germaine wanted to show Helen where she had found the locket and to check on Andrew McGrath's progress, so she went through a side gate to the back garden. Andrew McGrath was hard at work, but Germaine couldn't tell what he was doing. She cleared her throat and Andrew looked up, startled.

"Oh, Miss Germaine, I don't know what happened," Andrew said, distraught.

"What is it, Andrew?" she asked, concerned that the young boy was so upset.

"I don't know! Some squirrels or moles or something invaded the garden. Look at all these holes," he said, dropping his hands helplessly.

Germaine surveyed the damage and quickly understood that the holes were man-made.

"Andrew," Germaine said, "those holes were not dug by squirrels or moles. A human being with a shovel made those holes."

"Oh, Miss Germaine, it wasn't me! I would never dig up the garden like that! I'm working from North to South, just like you told me," cried Andrew.

"I know it wasn't you, Andrew. I know how proud you are of the work you are doing back here and would never sabotage it like that."

Andrew seemed to relax a bit under Germaine's reassurances. "I want you to think very carefully," she said to him seriously, "and tell me everyone with whom you have spoken about this job."

"Well, there's grandfather and grandmother of course," he said, using the fingers of one hand to indicate the people he began to list, "and I called my folks and my sister back in Ohio, and I guess the only other person I told is Pugsy. Pugsy Littleton, that is. He's the grandson of some of my grandparents' neighbors. He came over to visit the other night and we all played dominoes."

"And do you remember what you talked about when you met Pugsy?" Germaine asked.

"Well, he said he wanted to make some money this summer and I told him I was working for you in your garden. He said he wanted to do something easier, like delivering newspapers. My grandfather said he knew someone down at the Gazette office and he'd see what he could find out. Pugsy is a couple of years younger than me, so it would probably be hard for him to do real physical work like in your garden," Andrew said.

"Andrew, do you remember if you told Pugsy that you found things buried in the garden?"

"Why, yes, I did. I told him about the pottery shards and the snuff box. But he wouldn't have come here trying to steal things out of your garden, he's just a kid!" Andrew said, wrinkling his brow.

"He might have told someone else, Andrew," Germaine said, and the youth looked worried.

"Please don't blame yourself or think that you did anything wrong. But I would ask you not to mention the garden discoveries to anyone but your family from now on. Just to be safe," Germaine said, kindly.

"Oh Miss Germaine, I am so sorry! I promise I won't tell Pugsy or anyone else if we find more things back here."

Germaine smiled and realized she had completely forgotten that Helen Potter was standing behind her the whole time. She felt badly that she had chastised Andrew McGrath in front of a stranger. She introduced the two, and praised the fine job the youth was doing in the garden. She asked him in for lunch, but he said that he'd already been home to his grandparents' house for lunch. The two girls went inside as Andrew continued his work in the back yard.

"Gosh, Germaine," Helen said as the door to the kitchen closed. "Do you think a little boy really dug up all those holes?"

"It's certainly possible, but I wouldn't like to think a young boy would be so naughty," Germaine replied. "I just hope whoever it was didn't discover the old chest, or anything really important related to the locket. If all they found were some old pottery shards, I wouldn't mind so much."

"I shall certainly keep a very keen eye on what goes on in that garden," said Mrs. White, who had seen and heard the conversation in the garden, and was therefore preparing lunch for Germaine and Helen.

"Germaine, you always think the best of everyone. It's a very admirable quality, but I know the Littletons and they are a family of layabouts. If I see that boy of theirs anywhere near this garden, I'll send him packing," she said, slamming down the knife she was using to trim some fresh asparagus for emphasis.

As Mrs. White prepared lunch, Germaine explained how Andrew McGrath had come to be in Springdale for the summer and how his grandparents didn't want him to be idle for those few months. Helen noted that if he did a good job with her friend's garden, she might ask him to help her with some tasks around her house, which was on the other side of town. "Maybe he can specialize in nineteenth century gardening," she joked.

Mrs. White soon served a delicious meal of lightly steamed native asparagus, buttered egg noodles with almond slivers, and a salad of early local greens. As the girls ate, they discussed the mysterious locket and the "somber news" that Miss Rose had written about in her diary. Finally, Helen asked Germaine what she had meant by going on a treasure hunt.

"You said there was no digging involved, so I assume it wasn't the treasure hunt we just witnessed in the garden," Helen chuckled.

"Well," Germaine said bringing the dishes into the kitchen, "I was looking over the microfilm of the blueprints and plans of this house…"

"Isn't it great that they kept those? The whole Taylor Woods neighborhood is documented," said Germaine's friend.

"Yes, the Springdale Historical Society has always been so good about documentation," Germaine agreed. "In looking at the plans, I noticed that there were tiny marks on the blueprints. At first I thought they might be dust marks or flecks of something on the screen of the microfilm reader, but then I realized that two of them corresponded to secret compartments on two of the fireplaces."

"Secret compartments!" exclaimed Helen. "I didn't know you had secret compartments in your house! You never told me that! Are there hidden rooms and passageways, too? I'm jealous! All I have in my house is an old root cellar."

"There is at least one hidden room," Germaine smiled, "but I don't know about any secret passageways. You'll have to do the sleuthing to find it, if there is one."

"Really? You really have a hidden room?" Helen asked.

"Yes. I'll show it to you. But first, we have to look and see if we can find a third hidden compartment where the third asterisk was on the blueprints."

"Did you make a copy of the drawing?"

"No. But the other two marks were perfectly aligned to the hidden compartments in the fireplaces, so I expect that this third mark follows the same pattern."

"Where is it?" asked Helen, breathlessly.

"I'll show you," replied Germaine.

Chapter Eight: Hidden treasure

Little did the girls know, but their whole conversation had been overheard by Pugsy Littleton, who had stopped over to tease Andrew for working when he could have been relaxing and doing next to nothing all summer. Pugsy was just the sort of bad influence that Mr. McGrath feared his grandson would get involved with if he were idle all summer.

"Pugsy, you'd better get out of here right now. Miss Germaine thinks you dug up her garden and you're going to be in big trouble if she finds you here," Andrew said, not sure whether he thought the young boy had been really been so dishonest as to have dug in someone else's garden. Andrew knew that he would have to tell Germaine if Pugsy confessed that he had been sneaking around in her garden, and he worried that she would fire him. He didn't want to ask Pugsy directly if he'd been responsible for the holes.

"Oh relax, Andy," Pugsy said, trying to sound older and more confident than he really was. "She can't see me. Besides,

Germaine Moreau wouldn't hurt a fly. Mrs. White's the one to look out for," he said with a rather mean little grin.

Pugsy sat in the shade under the closed kitchen window while Andrew toiled in the sun. "But old Mrs. White doesn't even know I'm right here, under her nose."

"I wish you would leave, Pugsy. I don't want to tell on you, but I don't want Miss Germaine to fire me, either. I need this money for college."

"Hey, Andy," whispered Pugsy, "Germaine and Helen found a secret room in the house. Let's see if we can watch 'em without them noticing us. I think they're going in the basement. Maybe there's treasure hidden down there and we can find it first. Then neither of us would have to work all summer!"

"No way, Pugsy. Count me out. Miss Germaine has always been so nice to me. She'd fire me if she caught me sneaking around her house. Besides, it's just not right," said Andrew, resolutely.

Pugsy would not be attending college, and he thought nothing of eavesdropping or spying. In fact, he was hatching a scheme in his mind to snoop around the old Sheppard house when no one was home to see if he could find the secret room he had heard Germaine Moreau mention. He was sure it was full of gold coins and strings of pearls. He was already angry that he had spent a full hour digging in the garden and hadn't found anything except some old rocks, so he felt like he was owed a bigger treasure.

"Alright, already. I'll be seein' ya, then," said Pugsy, pretending to leave. "I can't believe you'd rather break your back in some lady's garden than pick up a big hidden treasure. If you change your mind, I'll be down at the river all afternoon."

Andrew turned back to his work, but little did he know that Pugsy had just snuck around the other side of the house and was peering into a basement window, straining to hear what the two girls were discussing.

"On one side of the chimney, there is a chute for the coal ashes to come down," explained Germaine, "but the architect was such a stickler for details, he must have thought that it would have looked odd to have that column be so much larger than the other, so they are the same size. The side where the ash pit is has an opening."

"And the other one doesn't, so that must be where the secret compartment is," Helen went on. "This G. Taylor Wood sure had a thing for symmetry, didn't he? I wonder if there are secret compartments like this in all the fireplaces on Beaumont Street?"

"Good question. Right now, I am only concerned about mine," answered Germaine as she poked and prodded at the bricks to the right of the chimney base. "Aha!" she exclaimed as one of the bricks came loose. "I found it."

Helen rushed to her friend's side and stood by breathlessly as Germaine felt around in the cavity. Both girls heard a muffled thud as Germaine's hand reached a hidden object.

"What is it? What do you feel? Is it square? Does it feel like a box?" Helen asked, practically jumping up and down.

As she did this, Pugsy Littleton pressed his face even closer to the basement window, but he still couldn't hear what Germaine and Helen said.

"I'm sure it is a box, Helen," Germaine said with anticipation.

Germaine pulled a large object wrapped in many layers of burlap from its niche. She walked over to an old wooden work table in the basement and placed the bundle down. She switched on an overhead light and began gently removing the layers of the coarse woven fabric. At last, she had taken away the last scrap and saw that the treasure was a small wooden box. Both Germaine and Helen let out a gasp. But as Germaine turned the box around in her hands she realized there was no locking mechanism. It was just a simple box with a lid. This was not the box that was opened by the key in the golden locket, but it was certainly interesting in its own right. The girls looked at each other as Germaine removed the lid. Then they looked at the contents. It was a stack of old letters, lovingly tied with a velvet ribbon.

"How exciting!" the two scholarly friends exclaimed in unison.

"Stupid letters!" spat Pugsy Littleton with manifest disgust. "Who cares? I thought it was gonna be pearls or gold or something. Awwwww shoot." And with that, Pugsy shuffled and kicked his way down to the river for an afternoon of fishing and napping.

"What was that?" Germaine said, holding up her hand.

"I didn't hear anything," Helen replied.

"I could have sworn I heard someone talking, right by the window."

"Maybe one of Andrew's friends stopped by," Helen said as she turned back towards the discovered treasure. "I'm sure it's nothing. Let's see what's in these, shall we?"

Helen made her way up to the library with the locket, the letters, and Germaine's notebook as Germaine helped Mrs. White make a pot of tea. Germaine brought the tea up to the library on an elegant silver tray, which she put down far from the precious old missives.

It was quickly apparent that the letters were several years' worth of correspondence between the two Sheppard sisters. Germaine knew a little bit about the Sheppard family from Springdale lore, and from stories her parents had passed down to her from the home's previous owner, Miss Rose Santini. Miss Rose's mother was Philippa Sheppard, who married a wealthy Italian count. Germaine recalled that there had been some sort of scandal about the marriage, but she couldn't remember just what the scandal concerned. The other sister, Miss Rose's aunt, was Lucetta Sheppard. The letters spanned several years, and the paper was brittle and spotted with age. The two researchers knew they would have to be very careful in handling them. They divvied up one stack, with Germaine taking Philippa's letters and Helen taking Lucetta's.

The girls gingerly smoothed down a few of the pages on the table. It was difficult to make out the writing on some of them, as the ink had faded and the paper had darkened over the years. Many of the letters contained mundane correspondence between two beloved sisters. There was discussion of the weather, their father's health, novels the girls were reading, and other family members. Then Helen found a letter from Philippa that was written on delicate blue onionskin paper and mailed from Italy. "Philippa's in Italy!" Helen exclaimed, and then read the letter aloud.

Dearest Lucetta, I barely know where to begin! Italy is beautiful — words do not suffice. We've been to the Temple of Vesta, to the Coliseum, the fountains, everywhere! Mrs. Lewis is a very good and thorough guide. She has taken Aunt Agatha and me everywhere and pointed out every site in her trusty Baedeker! One gets the sense that she never tires of showing her charges the same sites visit after visit. I do wish you were here with me dear Lucetta and that you hadn't felt so bound to stay in Springdale. Father could have done without you, you know.

How is everyone in Springdale? What a strange sensation it is to miss one place but feel so happy to be in another at the very same time. The light here is so pure and clear, Lucetta. I have done a bit of painting when I've had some time to myself. I would like so much to go out to one of the fields and set up my little easel and simply paint for an afternoon. The ruins are so suggestive of other times and remind us all how short are time here is.

I shall try to slip away to paint and will send you a little watercolor if I succeed! I love you so — I am hoping to receive word from you, my dearest sister.

Love to all, P.

"I wonder why Lucetta felt bound to stay in Springdale?" Helen asked.

"So do I. Let's read some more of these," Germaine replied.

They found more letters that indicated that the two sisters had been expected to go on this journey, part of the formation of all young American women of a certain social status in that era, but that Lucetta had cancelled, and Philippa feared it was because their father, Lyman Sheppard, asked her to stay stateside. Philippa met many charming English women and Americans.

"There is also a 'very generous' Italian count whose name is Lorenzo Santini. And she asks Lucetta about her two suitors, oo la la! This one is dated May twenty-third. Do you have any in your pile from Lucetta at about this time?" asked Helen.

Germaine skimmed through her letters until she found one that corresponded to that date. "She says that Horatio Fowler is terribly shy around her, but she very much enjoys his company. She then says that Colonel Bowles is being kinder, but she wishes he would be more respectful towards father."

"I wonder what that means?" Helen asked.

"I don't know," Germaine replied.

The girls continued reading, and from this long-forgotten correspondence between the Sheppard sisters, they were able to piece together some family history.

The older sister, Philippa, met Count Lorenzo Santini when she was in Italy. It was love at first sight, and although the Sheppard family was perfectly respectable, Count Santini was from an old and noble family, so his marrying Philippa disappointed many hopeful noblewomen in his country. His family had objections to his marrying beneath him; her family had objections to her marrying a foreigner and a Roman Catholic. But their love prevailed. They were married while Philippa was in Italy, but Lyman Sheppard, the family patriarch, was unhappy and his relationship with Philippa became strained, which pained her terribly. The Santinis moved into a modest cottage in Springdale, so as not to flaunt their wealth and social status, but they were seen as outsiders upon their return.

Lorenzo had to travel frequently for family business. He always returned with exquisite gifts of jewelry for Philippa, which set jealous tongues a flutter.

Meanwhile, Lucetta, the younger sister, was being courted by two men, the kind and gentle Horatio Fowler and the dashing Colonel Aubrey Bowles. Horatio was a clerk in their father Lyman's company. He was bookish and rather shy, but he was devoted to the lovely Lucetta. Their father frowned on this match, and Lucetta feared his disapproval, especially after Philippa's love match. Colonel Bowles was considered a better husband for Lucetta, but she didn't truly love him. She found him exciting and powerful, rather like their father Lyman, but she didn't feel the peace and joy in his presence that she felt with Horatio. Aubrey was from the socially prominent Bowles family, and Lucetta would have lots of social engagements to attend as his wife. She preferred the idea of a quiet home life with Horatio, reading books and walking in nature. However, she was a dutiful daughter and became engaged to the Colonel. Philippa felt somewhat responsible for her beloved sister's unhappy match; she thought Lucetta was choosing duty over love to make up for their father's disappointment in his oldest daughter's marriage.

"I never knew of this connection between the Bowles and Sheppard families," said Germaine, as she put down the letters and walked across the room to turn on a light. Night had fallen during the time the two friends were pouring over the old letters.

"Nor did I, and I'm supposed to be an expert on local genealogy. I wonder why it's not more widely known," mused Helen. "Do you think a Bowles descendent is the rightful heir to the locket?"

"That might be the case," Germaine replied, "but we have quite a few more letters to read through before we can make a decision. And besides, Claudia Saunders may still be correct that it was actually a Stevens locket and not a Sheppard locket at all!"

Although Germaine wanted to stay awake and continue reading on, she acquiesced to her friend's request and put the letters away for the day. Helen went home, and the two friends agreed to continue reading through the rest of the letters as soon as they could. Germaine decided to visit the Springdale Cemetery the following day to visit the Bowles and Sheppard gravesites and see if more information could be found there.

Chapter Nine: A mysterious stranger

The following day, Germaine arose early to prepare a report for Rodney Bennett about the floorcloths he was interested in procuring. She looked out an upstairs window overlooking the garden and was dismayed to see more holes in the garden. Andrew hadn't arrived yet, and she feared that his little friend Pugsy might have been digging up the garden again in hopes of finding more treasures. While she would be interested in finding anything the garden might yield, she did not want anyone else to discover the box that matched the tiny key she had found in the locket. She was determined to give everything to the rightful heirs of the locket, be they Stevenses, Sheppards, Santinis or someone else entirely. There were only a few holes this morning, and they seemed shallower than the first batch, so she hoped the young treasure-hunter had given in to what seemed to be his natural idleness and abandoned the idea.

After she completed Mr. Bennett's report, she put on some sensible walking shoes and prepared a bagged lunch to bring to the Springdale Cemetery. It was a walk of many blocks and the trip brought Germaine through several of the interesting neighborhoods filled with historic homes that Springdale was famous for. It was a lovely sunny day, and Germaine left the house with a spring in her step.

By the time she left, Andrew was hard at work in the garden, and Germaine realized how pleased she was that she'd taken on the McGrath's grandson to do the needed work in the garden. He was doing a fine job of it, and it freed Germaine up to do her historical decorating and to do the sleuthing that had so occupied her since the discovery of the locket.

She slipped the Rodney Bennett report into the first mailbox she came to. As she continued on her way, she thought of all the names with the initials LS that she had discovered; but which among them had the important second S? There was Lyman Sheppard, the Sheppard family paterfamilias. The photographs could have been of his two daughters. Still, the locket was a woman's ornament and unlikely to have been worn by a man. Perhaps his wife Edith had worn the necklace with his initials? Then there was Lucetta Sheppard. It could have been her and her sister or her sister and mother. And then there was

Lorenzo Santini. He talked a lot about jewels and jewelry in his letters. Maybe it was his locket, or his initials. And Claudia might have been absolutely correct that Lewis Stanley Stevens had lived there and the photos might have been of his wife and daughter. There were so many possibilities! Germaine let out a big sigh, and as she did, realized she wasn't paying any attention to the beautiful old homes she was walking past, so she put the thoughts of the initials out of her mind and concentrated on her surroundings.

And she was pleased she did. Germaine walked past block after block of well-preserved and well-loved homes, some dating back as far as the Colonial era. These few homes from the early 1700s had often been added to over the years, but their original footprint was usually visible, especially to someone with Germaine Moreau's trained eye. She enjoyed counting panes of glass in windows to help determine in what era a home had been constructed, and she smiled as she noted the twelve over twelve panes of those early homes. There were also Federal-era homes from the early 1800s, many of which had six over six panes of glass. But most of the most impressive homes throughout

Springdale were Victorians, like the Sheppard House on Beaumont Street, which dated from the mid 1800's through the early 1900's, and had only one or two panes of glass on each window. The homes grew more ornate and extravagant as she neared the cemetery. Some houses had three turrets, each in a different shape. Many had decorative cast iron scrollwork, and others still featured working exterior gaslights. Germaine's historical decoration work and social connections had brought her inside many of these stately homes, and she was able to recall many of the special features of the houses as she walked past, thanks to her nearly photographic memory.

Finally, Germaine reached the cemetery. The entrance to the cemetery was not prominent, and many visitors looking for the place drove right past it. There were two simple brownstone columns flanking a long allee of elms and sycamores. Arching between the two columns was a simple cast iron sign that read "Springdale Cemetery." A small brass plaque on one of the columns informed visitors that the gates to the cemetery opened at eight o'clock each morning and closed at dusk. Germaine always found this vague closing time somewhat unsettling, and more than once worried that she would be locked in the cemetery if her research among the old headstones kept her there in the late afternoon. Luckily, there would be no danger of an accidental locking in on this trip; it was not even noon yet, and she knew just where she was going.

Germaine had been visiting the impressive Springdale Cemetery since she was a little girl. Many of her family members were buried there, and she also used to accompany her parents to the grounds when they had research to conduct. The site had originally been an Indian burial ground, and when the colonists arrived, they began sharing the space with the original inhabitants, until the Europeans eventually took over. There were three headstones of Springdale residents dating back to the 1600s, but the grounds were given their distinctive layout by noted landscape architect Francis Burke-Ley during the Civil War, when so many of Springdale's young men were killed. Burke-Ley had a finely-tuned sense of aesthetics, and despite the sad function of his design, the form was beautiful. The most prominent Springdale citizens took it upon themselves to choose prime plots when the cemetery was first designed, and the

Sheppard plot had a location that made the family's importance quite clear. They spent their eternal rest on a small hill, in an extremely pleasant and shady corner of the grounds. The Sheppard plot featured a subtle granite obelisk in the center, with a few smaller grave markers nearby. The plot itself was delineated by a simple cast iron fence and gate with the initial "S" on a shield in the middle of it.

Germaine pushed open the gate and took out her notebook and pencil as she approached the obelisk. The names of the deceased Sheppard family members were engraved on the obelisk, along with their years of birth and death and their relationship to the patriarch.

Lyman Samuel Sheppard, husband and father

Agnes, wife

Samuel, son

Edith, wife

Philippa, daughter

Lucetta, daughter

Germaine was somewhat surprised to learn that Lyman had married twice and had lost an infant son. While both were common occurrences, she thought she knew of all the Sheppard family members.

"First a Bowles in the family and now a second wife. I wonder what other surprises await me?" Germaine asked herself as she wrote down all the information from the grave marker. As she came to the daughters, she noted that neither Philippa's nor Lucetta's spouse was listed on the stone, and the sisters' last names were also omitted.

"I wonder why Lyman disliked his sons-in-law so much?" she mused. Germaine was eager to return to the history museum to do more research on the former inhabitants of her home. She had lots of questions and hoped her friend Helen would help her find the information she needed. Before she left, Germaine took a quick glance at the names on the other, smaller headstones within the confines of the Sheppard family's fenced plot. The names and dates indicated other Sheppard family members – aunts, cousins, a sister of Lyman, but nothing that struck Germaine as especially significant. Still, she noted all these names and dates on another piece of paper.

She closed the gate and noticed a very modest headstone behind the Sheppard plot. It read "Lorenzo S. Santini." The grass had grown rather high around the stone, and Germaine thought she saw more engraving behind the grass. She pushed it out of the way and read "*Wronged*" engraved in a different font and style than the name and date. Germaine was so surprised that she rocked backwards and found herself sitting on the ground. "Wronged?" she asked herself. "What could it mean?"

As she jotted down the information on Lorenzo's stone, she stopped. "Lorenzo S. Santini. LSS!" Germaine exclaimed. She sketched the stone out to show to Helen. "I wish I had paid closer attention when my parents told me about the Sheppards and Santinis," she said wistfully. She put her notebook down and noticed a small stone beside Lorenzo Santini's. It was the small, quiet marker for Rose Santini. She put her hand upon Miss Rose's name.

"Do you know how that locket got in your yard, Miss Rose?" Germaine wondered aloud. She sat for what seemed like a very long time wondering how the locket, the letters, the journal entry, and the single word *"Wronged"* engraved on a tombstone could all be related. As she sat there lost in thought, she was jarred back into the present by an old man speaking to her. "Funny, ain't it, Miss," said a clipped, Yankee voice. "No-one really knows who had that engraved." Germaine looked up and saw an elderly groundskeeper leaning on a rake. "Are you going to try to figure it out, too?" he asked with a bemused smile.

"What do you mean 'too'," asked Germaine as she stood up and brushed the grass off her trousers.

"Young man, 'bout your age, was here a few days ago, spent hours looking at the Sheppard's and Bowles' plots. He had a notebook just like that one, too. Must've bought 'em at the same store. Heh," chuckled the caretaker.

Germaine's notebook was the type used by historians and researchers. It was made with special paper, and had a distinctive orange cover. She knew that if the other person researching the family had possessed the same notebook, he was a professional historian, too.

"Would you be so kind as to point me in the direction of the Bowles' plot?" asked Germaine politely.

"Ayuh," replied the worker. "It's not in such a nice stretch as these graves here. Go down the road until you see a great big monument shaped like a ship. That's where Captain Charles Day and his son Sergeant William Day are buried. Take a left at that corner, and the Bowles plot you want is in that section. They have an urn draped with a veil."

"I know just where the ship is, thank you," Germaine replied and started making her way towards the area indicated. Her mind was racing with questions, but the one uppermost in her thoughts was who else was researching the same families, and might that person be the legitimate heir to the golden locket. She so hoped to be able to return the locket to its rightful heir that she became very excited at the prospect. "Perhaps that Aubrey Bowles who is running for Senate in Chalmsford is related to the Sheppards," she thought, acknowledging that Bowles was not an uncommon name in New England.

Germaine made her way past the very impressive ship monument, which told the story of how Captain Day had fought off the Royal British Navy, even though he was outnumbered, and saved the lives of hundreds of men during the War of 1812. He lived to be a ripe old age, and his son was also a heroic sailor. It had been one of her favorite monuments as a child, but she had never really noticed the rather meager draped urn a few plots behind it. It was the grave of Colonel Aubrey Bowles. Germaine remembered a class she had taken on Victorian iconography that proposed that draped or veiled headstones represented an unconscious desire on the survivors to hide something about the deceased.

"I wonder if Colonel Bowles' descendants wished to hide something about him," she mused. As she began to take her notebook and pencil out to jot down the information on the Bowles' headstone, she was startled by a sudden noise behind her.

Germaine turned just in time to see a man walking very briskly away from her. The noonday sun was shining directly overhead, yet she couldn't quite get a fix on his form. He was walking in a distinctly unnatural manner. It immediately flashed into Germaine's mind that the man was deliberately altering his stride. But why? Germaine called out to him, but the stranger simply raised his left hand in a salute as he raced away. Germaine looked around for the groundskeeper, but couldn't see him. She decided he must be at lunch, and realized that she ought to eat soon, too. She remembered the sandwiches and thermos of lemonade she had packed for herself, and decided to eat as soon as she had written down the information on the Bowles' markers.

Tucking her notebook under her arm, and picking up her satchel, Germaine made her way to the Lionel Lachance Temple. That was not the monument's official name, but one that Springdale natives had given the final resting place of one of their noteworthy citizens. The location in question was an elegant Greek rotunda with slender Doric columns in a peaceful, shady area of the cemetery. It was dedicated to the memory of Lionel Lachance, a French Canadian émigré who had made a fortune in marble, and it was constructed of the finest specimens of that material. While unassuming when seen from afar, closer inspection revealed that the columns and dome were made of solid Carrera marble, while upon the granite foundation was a mosaic representing the composition of the evening sky on the night Lionel Lachance exited this world. The stars were inlaid in solid gold, and the sky was formed by precious lapis lazuli and onyx. The marble exterior was slowly eroding with time, but the celestial chart looked much as it must have when it was created. It was one of Germaine's favorite places to repose, so she climbed the few steps to the monument and sat with her back against a column, enjoying the cool feel of the marble against her back.

As Germaine lunched, she pondered over the many strange events that had happened since she found that mysterious golden locket. She was quite preoccupied with finding the rightful owner, but had uncovered so many other unexpected pieces of information on the way to that end. At the moment, she was truly stumped by the many bearers of the initials "LSS" and wondered if she would ever discover just whose locket the locket was. She finished up her lunch, put the sandwich wrapper back in her bag, and made sure she hadn't left any litter behind.

"I must get to the museum and consult with Helen," she said as she stood up. And with that, she made her way out of the cemetery, and fortunately found a taxi passing by just as she exited the gates. She hopped in and in a few minutes was paying the driver in front of the entrance to the Springdale Historical Museum.

Chapter Ten: A fortune foretold?

Germaine found an empty space at one of the long tables in the basement archive section of the Historical Society, and was just about to take a seat when Helen Porter rushed up to her with a strange look on her face. "Germaine," she said breathlessly, "someone else has been researching the Bowles and Sheppard families…and you'll never guess who it is!"

"Chauncey Fetterson?" replied Germaine with a smile.

Helen was flabbergasted. "How did you know?"

"I was at the cemetery today looking at the two families' grave sites, and there was a strange figure there. There was something familiar about the man, even though he disguised his appearance. When I remembered that Chauncey had been here earlier this week, I realized it was he. He tried to use a strange walk and wore a hat over his face. But what I don't know is why he disguised himself and why he was researching these same intertwined families. Did he reveal anything to you?"

"No," replied Helen. "And he was very brusque with me when I asked him what he was up to. He basically told me it was none of my business. He just left a few minutes before you arrived."

"When I was in Chalmsford the other day my fortune cookie read 'someone close is deceiving you', maybe the fortune was true," she said, jokingly.

"Oh Germaine, you don't believe in fortune cookies," Helen said, knowing her friend was not at all superstitious.

"No, of course I don't, but I do feel like Chauncey is avoiding us and I really can't fathom why he would disguise himself like that."

"Well, I kept all the documents he requested out for you. I'll bring them over. Maybe you can figure out what he was looking for."

As Germaine poured over the records of the Sheppard and Bowles family, the story that she had gleaned from Lucetta and Philippa's letters was confirmed. Philippa married Lorenzo Santini in Italy and when they returned here, they moved to a small cottage near the river. Their daughter Rose was born a few years later, and after Lyman Sheppard died, the Santini family moved into the Sheppard home on Beaumont Street. Lucetta married Colonel Aubrey Bowles and after some years living in Springdale, they moved to Boston. They had two children; a daughter Viola and a son, Aubrey Junior, who was the father of Aubrey III, now running for the Senate. Even though the Bowles family had moved to Boston in the previous century, they still used the burial plot in Springdale; this was a not-uncommon practice, as burial in the Springdale Cemetery was considered quite prestigious.

Germaine reviewed the notes she had made as she read through the large pile of documents that Helen gave her. So far, everything matched up with the Sheppard sisters' letters. It seemed likely that the Bowles family would indeed be the rightful heirs of any discovered Sheppard property, since Miss Rose Santini had never had children. Germaine shared her findings with Helen, but stressed that she needed conclusive proof that it was a Sheppard or Santini, and not a Stevens who had once owned the mysterious golden locket.

"No matter who originally owned it, Germaine, you are now the rightful owner in the eyes of the law," Helen told her friend matter-of-factly.

"Oh, but just imagine if your family had an heirloom floating around somewhere, Helen. Wouldn't you want it back in the family if someone found it?" Germaine asked.

"I suppose. But I bet not many people who found a $50,000 golden locket that was legally theirs would try to give it away," Helen responded.

As she made her way home from the museum, Germaine mulled over the records she had found in the history museum, and wondered what Chauncey had been looking for and why he had behaved so oddly in the cemetery. She decided to call on him the following day, but she would not mention the golden locket unless Chauncey brought up the topic. She debated with herself about telling her old friend the whole story.

"His behavior has been very peculiar," she thought, "I suppose he is under a great deal of stress finishing up Symphony Hall, but I can't understand why he pretended not to recognize me in the cemetery."

Germaine decided she would listen to Chauncey's explanation of his trip to the cemetery before she shared all her information. In the meantime, she wanted to finish reading the sisters' letters. She also hoped to discover the location of the box that the key opened, so that she could pass that along to the rightful heir, along with the locket and key.

The telephone was ringing as Germaine entered her home. Mrs. White was gone for the day, so she sat down at the telephone table and lifted up the receiver. Edward Bartlett was on the other end.

"Germaine dear," said the kindly family friend, "how's your investigation proceeding?"

Germaine caught her friend up with the story so far, and added, "What would you think if I told you Aubrey Bowles III might be the rightful heir to the locket?"

"Hah!" Edward Bartlett snorted, "I shouldn't like to see that character get his hands on fine jewelry like that locket. He'd probably melt it down and make a money clip out of it. Possession is nine-tenths of the law, child. I know you are determined to find some worthy soul to give the locket to, but if the soul turns out not to be so worthy, you could always donate it to a museum."

"You sound like Helen," Germaine said gently. "We don't know anything definitive yet. And I have stacks more letters to read. I'm going to call on Chauncey tomorrow, but I shan't say anything about the locket. I want to learn more about what he's up to first."

"Well I've got something to show you that might just be related to the locket and the key. Want to see it?"

"Of course! What is it?" she asked with great anticipation.

"I'd rather show you than tell you. I'm off to New York tomorrow for a few days, but I can call at your place on my way home. I think you will be quite interested in what I have found," he said before putting the phone down.

Chapter Eleven: 27 Trilby Street

"Would you please be patient?" asked a man's exasperated voice. Germaine had just pulled the old-fashioned manual doorbell at 27 Trilby Street. She could hear muttering and shuffling of papers on the other side of the door as she did as instructed and waited patiently for it to be opened.

"Oh. Germaine." Chauncey Fetterson said this with a slightly furrowed brow.

"Hello Chauncey," Germaine greeted her friend with a charming smile. "Long time no see! I am given to understand that we are researching the same old Springdale families, and I thought we could compare notes," she said as she maneuvered her way inside, just in case Chauncey decided to bar her entrance.

Germaine scanned the dining room table of the elegantly cluttered brownstone townhouse Chauncey called home. She knew that the dining room table was what he called his "headquarters," and she remembered how commodious it was when Germaine, Helen, and Chauncey all studied at it together during their college days. She hoped to get a glimpse of whatever paperwork Chauncey might have on the Sheppards. There were stacks of paper everywhere, most held in place with large crystal paperweights. There was too much paper to make heads or tails of it from a distance.

"May I sit?" she asked, motioning to an empty chair at headquarters.

"I don't suppose I can stop you," her friend sighed.

"Well, if you aren't going to offer me a glass of lemonade or something, I suppose I'll just get started with the questions," she said perkily.

Chauncey sighed again and shuffled off into the Butler's Pantry to squeeze some lemons. Chauncey's love for homemade lemonade and his authentic Edwardian recipe for the simple drink had infected his two friends. Whenever the three socialized together in the warm months, they always made pitchers of it.

As Chauncey started the rather labor-intensive process, Germaine scanned the stacks of papers strewn across his dining room table. She lifted up the paperweights and saw piles of documents dedicated to Spanish silver hallmarks, ivory handled walking sticks, Lucite punch bowls, Spiritualism, bookplates, the image of the wanderer in eighteenth-century English poetry, and carved New England granite grave markers. "Hmmmm," murmured Germaine as she delved deeper into that particular stack of papers. She found images of large and ornate grave markers from the Victorian era: Daguerreotypes, tintype prints, etchings and early photographs from British and American cemeteries, all examples of exceptionally large grave markers. There were urns, obelisks, statues, and geometric shapes. Beneath the photographs, Germaine caught a glimpse of a sketch of a very elaborate mausoleum with the initial B emblazoned across the top of it.

"It looks like you've got an interesting batch of work on your plate," Germaine said as the door between the Butler's Pantry and dining room swung open.

"That's one way to look at it," said Chauncey, as he deliberately placed an ebonized tray on top of the pile of papers Germaine had just been riffling through. The tray held Chauncey's freshly made lemonade and some shortbread cookies that Germaine recognized as having come from the kitchen of Chauncey's father, a renowned Scottish baker. Her friend then stood before a carved breakfront that took up one entire wall in the dining room and took down two hand-blown Elizabethan goblets and two Sevres porcelain plates with a bold star motif. He found finely loomed linen napkins in one of the drawers and placed the settings before his guest and his self.

"Look Germaine," Chauncey said in brusquely, "what do you want? I'm sure Helen told you I've been doing research at the museum, but it doesn't concern you at all."

"My goodness, Chauncey, your father's baking just gets better and better!" exclaimed Germaine, in an attempt to disarm her friend. "And you have simply perfected your lemonade recipe."

"It doesn't concern you!"

"You know, Chauncey," Germaine went on, watching her friend for his reaction, "I was at the Springdale Cemetery today. It's so beautiful. Have you been recently? The groundskeeper does such a good job. And he's such a helpful chap."

Chauncey's eyes blazed, but he said nothing.

"I was there because I am doing research on the Sheppard family. You know, they were the original owners and namesakes of my home, Sheppard House."

"I know, I know. You were always so smitten with your parents' stories about that house."

"I thought I knew them all. But I just learned that a Sheppard was married to a Bowles. To Colonel Aubrey Bowles. The grandfather of the Aubrey Bowles who is running for Senate," as she let this statement sink in, she sunk back into her chair to watch for Chauncey's reaction. "Did you know that?"

Chauncey started coughing and choking on his shortbread cookie. Germaine lifted her eyebrows and tilted her head in such a way to ask if he needed help, but he waved her away and managed to regain his composure.

"Yes, I did know that, Germaine. Look, I'm doing some research and design work for the Bowles family that has nothing to do with your precious Sheppards and Santinis, or if it does, it's only in the most tangential way," Chauncey said, sternly.

Germaine sipped her lemonade and said nothing. She looked at Chauncey with a placid smile on her face.

"Stop looking at me like that," he requested, to no avail. "Okay fine. I'll tell you, and I know you'll tell Helen, but it stops there. You can't let anyone else know. I expect you to honor that request on the basis of our long friendship," he said rather solemnly.

"Good heavens, Chauncey, this sounds serious!"

"Aubrey Bowles – the current one – thinks his family grave is too modest. He's commissioned me to design a new mausoleum for the family. They're going to disinter the bodies and put them in the new structure. But they want it to be as quiet as possible. They've hired me to design something that will look authentically Victorian, and they're even going to bang it up a bit so that it looks like it's always been there," he said, sheepishly.

This time it was Germaine who nearly choked. "Oh Chauncey," she said between gasps of laughter, "that is one of the most ridiculous things I have ever heard!

"And that is why you were behaving so oddly at the cemetery and the museum?" she went on.

"I got nervous when I saw you. This isn't exactly a project that I'd like to brag about; not to mention that I've been sworn to secrecy… I figured I would try to escape your astute questions, but I should have known you would discover what I was up to sooner or later."

"But everyone will know," she went on. "You can't just plop a huge granite mausoleum down in the middle of the cemetery without anyone noticing. What is he thinking?"

"He's thinking that he's going to do it over Labor Day weekend when most people are out of town, and no one will notice. He figures that even if the local historians notice the new structure, they aren't important and no one will listen to them. He wants to use it in his campaign to show his long roots in the community," and with this even Chauncey started chuckling.

"I still have to work for a living, so I took the job," Chauncey went on. "I had no idea it was going to be this absurd, but here we are," he said with a smile. "The Symphony Hall project was winding up and I thought it might be an interesting challenge."

"From Symphony Hall to the Springdale Cemetery, you'll have your name on buildings all over the city," Germaine said in a mixture of teasing and admiration.

"Only no one will know about this one, right?" Chauncey asked, raising his eyebrow.

"I promise. I won't tell anyone but Helen, and I shall swear her to secrecy."

"And what exactly are you doing researching the Sheppards?" Chauncey went on, relieved not to keep a secret from his two friends anymore.

"Just curious about some local history," she said, without disclosing the full story.

"I'll admit, I was surprised when I found that Sheppard-Bowles connection," Chauncey said. "I haven't brought it up with A.B.3. – that's what his confidants call him, don't you know – and he hasn't mentioned it; but it was news to me."

"Hmm... I wonder why the Bowles would shun their association with the Sheppards if they're trying to show how long they've been part of the community?" mused Germaine.

"Perhaps Aubrey doesn't know he's a Sheppard. I'm sure he'd be trumpeting it in his radio spots if he did know. The family had such a good reputation, and Miss Rose Santini was a major philanthropist.

"But tell me more about your research, Germaine. 'Local history' is a broad topic. Are you trying to hide something from me yourself?" he asked.

Germaine told Chauncey about the letters the girls had found, and she shared *most* of their contents with her friend, but she omitted the discovery of the locket, the key, and the other jewels that were alluded to in the letters. She was not sure why she didn't tell her old friend everything she had discovered, but she thought it was somehow better to wait until she had finished reading the sisters' hidden correspondence and she had a more complete picture of the situation.

Chapter Twelve: Siblings' Letters

"And it's going to be installed over Labor Day when fewer people will be around, so that no one will notice" Germaine told Helen, sharing Chauncy Fetterson's explanation of the Bowles work.

"But everyone will notice. How can they think that no one will notice an enormous mausoleum where the day before only a humble draped urn stood?" she asked.

"They clearly have little consideration of the wisdowm of the general populous, which seems a poor characteristic for a public servant. Chauncey said they figured the only people who would notice were historians, and we don't matter."

Helen expressed her disagreement as she put down the cup of tea she had been enjoying in Germaine's music room. Mrs. White had made a rhubarb pie the previous day and the girls were enjoying a restorative snack before delving into the rest of the letters. They soon finished and made their way back up to the library, where they'd left the letters a few days ago.

Germaine continued on with Philippa's letters and Helen with Lucetta's. The girls read the old correspondence for quite some time, the silence broken only by the crinkle of old paper. Each had an orange historian's notebook by her side, occasionally scribbling notes that might prove to be important in their research. At last, Germaine found a letter that stood out from all the others. "Oh Helen," she exclaimed, "Aubrey Bowles was going around to the important families in Springdale insinuating that Lorenzo Santini was a jewel thief!"

"Good heavens!" Helen could barely believe it. "What is the date of that letter?"

Germaine was a faster reader than her friend, so Helen had to put aside some of her stack of missives until she came to the same time period. The friends read through the sisters' correspondence from this era and learned that whenever Lorenzo Santini was out of town on family business, there was a major jewel theft somewhere on the East Coast. And when Santini came back to Springdale from his trips, he always presented Philippa with a spectacular gift of expensive jewelry. Aubrey Bowles started gossiping that Santini wasn't really going out on family business at all, that he was a sneaking jewel thief, and that he was not to be trusted.

Dearest Philippa, I am so distraught, but can only imagine that your distress greatly exceeds my own. Aubrey has been telling Franklin Rice that Lorenzo stole Margaret Frederick's jewels in Philadelphia. His argument is quite convincing, I'm sorry to say. I overheard him telling Franklin that Lorenzo was out of town when Mrs. Frederick's things were taken, and then he laid out a whole set of other times when Lorenzo was away and ladies had their things taken. Oh Philippa, I don't know what to believe. Lorenzo seems so good and kind and gentlemanly. I can't imagine he would be wooing wealthy widows behind your back, but Aubrey's case is so convincing. Oh Philippa, Philippa....

Your own dearest friend and sister,

Lucetta

"What a dreadful situation for everyone involved," Germaine said with compassion. "But Philippa's faith in her husband never wavered. Listen to her response."

Oh Lucetta, my sister, my light, Lorenzo is not a thief. He is incapable of deception of any sort, and he is as true and dear to me as you are, beloved sister. My husband is half of my very soul, and you know that I would never do such a thing, so you should know that he never would either. I am untroubled by your husband's claims, the only worry that crosses my brow is for you, dear. I cannot imagine why Aubrey is making such outrageous accusations, and doing so in such an ungentlemanly fashion. If he wants to accuse my Lorenzo of theft, why does he not do so frankly and openly, rather than going about whispering in men's ears? Poor Lucetta, to be in such a home with such a man. Oh, how I wish you had wed that dear Mr. Fowler. Did I tell you he stopped by last month to call upon us? He was so good and kind with little Rose... Ah well, what is done is done.

Goodbye for now my dear,

Philippa

"She has a point," said Helen. "Why didn't the Colonel go to the police, or at least speak directly to Lorenzo? All that whispering is indeed ungentlemanly, and behavior unbecoming to an officer, if you ask me. Some chivalrous officer he," Helen sniffed, disapprovingly.

"In the Victorian era, families of good standing only wanted to see their names in the papers to announce a marriage or a death," Germaine said, repeating an axiom often quoted by Dr. Laura Peterson, one of their favorite professors at Elmhurst College.

"I know, but still…" Helen said. "These are very serious accusations to be making behind Lorenzo's back."

"Here's Lucetta's response," Germaine said, holding the letter aloft.

Dearest Philippa, I don't know what to do; I am nearing my wits' end. Aubrey continues with his gossip and accusations of Lorenzo. I don't even like to tell you that it's happening, but I feel somehow I must. Philippa, dear, couldn't we just go away, you and I? We could go off to France or to Poland, somewhere quiet and simple. I don't want to see your name in the newspaper about this, or poor father's name, or that of any Sheppard. I simply don't know what to do. I am paralyzed. I dare not speak against Aubrey, he flies into such a black and bitter rage when I contradict him. Could we go off to Europe together, dearest? I haven't any money of my own, and Aubrey says we've none to spare. He is so busy with the orphanage he is funding, that it takes all his time and money. See, Philippa, what a good man he is? How could someone be bad if he is creating a home for the poor little children of Boston? Could you pay for my ticket? Perhaps you could ask father for the money for my travel. Or Lorenzo? Oh, it's all too sordid. Philippa, darling, either your husband is a thief or mine is a slanderer. Can't we get away from this?

Your desperate sister.

"That does sound desperate," Helen agreed solemnly. "But also a little sneaky; she seems to be asking if Philippa has seen any hidden stashes of money around. I wonder if Lorenzo really was stealing jewelry?"

"And I wonder what happened to the orphanage Aubrey Bowles was allegedly constructing. Ever hear of it?" Germaine asked.

"No … now that you mention it, I haven't," Helen responded.

"Nor have I," Germaine concurred. "I'm adding it to our list of research items, which grows each day," she added with a smile.

Germaine and Helen sympathized with the sisters' predicaments. "But surely the jewels would have been recognized by their rightful owners if Philippa wore them in public. If they really were stolen, that is," mused Helen.

"Not necessarily," replied Germaine, betraying the shrewdness of her intellect. "The first theft mentioned was in Philadelphia. Besides, if Lorenzo was stealing jewels from people's homes in Springdale, he wouldn't have been foolish enough to give them to Philippa. He could have either sold them and bought her other gems, or he could have had a jeweler re-work the stones into different settings."

"I remember your telling me that Edward Bartlett thought that the key pre-dated the locket. Perhaps Lorenzo had a bunch of stolen gold melted down and made into a locket for Philippa, and put the key in as a token of his affection," Helen said, giving words to a thought that Germaine had already considered.

"Helen, do you remember those stories about a fake Italian count who wooed widows in Boston and New York and then got them to turn over their finest jewels to him before he left and broke their hearts?" asked Germaine.

"Now that you mention it, I vaguely remember reading about it in our class on Victorian crime. Do you think it could have been Lorenzo Santini?"

"I'm not sure. From what I remember, this man used a different name each time, but the confidence trick he played was the same in each instance. He gave the widows elaborate gifts of jewelry, showered them with attention, had huge bouquets of flowers delivered every day, took them out to all the fine restaurants and shows of the time, and then convinced them to have all their old jewelry re-set into more modern fashions by a jeweler friend of his."

"And once they handed over the jewels, they never saw them again."

"Correct. And it turned out that the jewels he'd given the women were paste, the flowers were taken from funeral homes, and the restaurant tabs were never paid. The ladies were so embarrassed that they seldom pressed charges, but when their children found out that part of their inheritance had been robbed, then the police were called in," Germaine said, displaying her recollection of the long-forgotten story.

"Was the thief ever caught?" asked Helen, who couldn't remember the class as well as her friend.

"No. He used a different name and phony noble title each time. And if I'm not mistaken, the names all had something in common, but I can't remember what it was."

"Well for once, we both can't remember something. I wish it wasn't so late; we'll have to wait until tomorrow to look over the newspaper archives to see if we can link Lorenzo Santini to this crime wave. Although marrying Philippa and living happily in a cottage here in Springdale doesn't seem to be quite in keeping with the character of a con artist," said Helen.

"No, it doesn't," Germaine answered thoughtfully. The young woman was putting together an alternate theory in her mind. "May I read some of those letters of Lucetta's from the same time, please?"

After reading a few of the letters Philippa had written to her sister, Germaine put the stack down and stared out the window. She took up her notebook and carefully wrote several entries, underlining words here and there. Helen didn't interrupt her friend, but she did wonder what Germaine was writing.

Chapter Thirteen: The Swarthy Swiper

"Aha!" Germaine exclaimed as she zoomed in on yet another front page of the New York *Tribune* at her microfilm station.

"Which name did he use this time?" asked Helen, who was searching through the Boston *Post* microfilms of the same year

"Count Luca Sappone of Capri," answered Germaine.

"We'll add that to Duke Leonardo Sarto, Duke Luigi Scotello, Lino di Sorrento, Count Lippo Scoiattolo of Naples, and Count Ludovico Scimmio. They're all names with the initials LS, but never include Lorenzo or Santini," Helen noted. "Germaine, you studied Italian in college. Do any of the names mean anything?"

"Soap, tailor, squirrel, monkey, and knife," answered Germaine matter-of-factly. "Although some Italian names mean certain things such as locations or professions, sort of like the

English surname 'Baker' or 'West,'" I think that these names are all made up."

"Does 'Santini' mean anything?" asked Helen.

"Little saints," Germaine answered. "But like 'Sarto,' which means tailor, it's a legitimate last name."

"Well that's just despicable. Lorenzo Santini was adding insult to injury by making up these silly names when he robbed those vulnerable widows."

"Hold on. I don't think it was Lorenzo Santini at all," Germaine said, much to Helen's surprise. "I think the robber took advantage of the low esteem in which Italians, especially southern Italians, were held here in America at that time. The thief was always described as swarthy and oily, and always said he came from some southern Italian location like Sorrento, or Capri or Naples. The newspapers always report his accent as very peculiar and that his English was hard to understand.

"The real Lorenzo Santini was an accomplished polyglot. He spoke fluent German, Dutch, Flemish, French, and Spanish, in addition to Italian and English. None of the sisters' letters state that he was difficult to understand, and in his letters to Philippa from abroad, his English is impeccable." Germaine concluded.

"But he was disguising himself!" Helen said, sure that Lorenzo Santini was the Swarthy Swiper of the tabloids.

"Lorenzo Santini was very proud of being Italian and he likely had to contend with ugly stereotypes in this country regularly. If he were to pretend to be someone else, why not a German or a Spaniard?" Germaine quizzed her friend. "And why would he cast suspicion on himself by using the same initials as his own name?"

"Crooks do that all the time. They secretly want to proclaim their cleverness in what they've gotten away with, but don't want to be caught, so they disguise themselves incompletely, or they use a similar type of name, or leave other such clues behind. You'd be surprised at some of the things that give people away in the codes I've seen as a cryptologist."

"Perhaps," replied Germaine, "but I am sure that the thief was *not* Lorenzo Santini."

Germaine motioned for her friend to join her at her microfilm station. As Helen positioned her chair in front of the useful machine, Germaine zoomed in to several artists' renderings of the Swarthy Swiper in the New York newspapers of the time that had frequently reported these crimes. He was always depicted as a short dark man with small, darting eyes, a thin moustache and a bit of a pot belly. Then Germaine took an envelope that contained a fragile *carte de visite* and an old photograph out of her briefcase. She placed both artifacts on the table before her. She pointed to the man in the photos and asked her friend if she saw any resemblance between the tall, fair, and noble face in the photos and the small and mean face in the newspapers. Helen admitted she did not. Then Germaine pulled that day's Springdale *Gazette* out of her bag and opened it to an advertisement.

"Do you see any resemblance here?" she asked, placing the newspaper beside the microfiche viewer.

Her friend gasped, "Aubrey Bowles! He looks just like the Swiper!"

"Would that be the Swarthy Swiper?" asked a familiar voice. It was Chauncey Fetterson. Germaine and Helen quickly exchanged a look. The girls silently wondered if they could trust their old college chum with their discovery, given his relationship with the Bowles family.

"I remember reading about old Swarthy in our High Society and High Crimes class. A fake Italian count who made off with wealthy widows' wares up and down the East Coast, if I remember correctly," Chauncey went on, unaware of the girls' supposition of the Swarthy Swiper's true identity.

"I say!" said Chauncey, "That's an enormous locket! Have you two stumbled upon the Swiper's loot or something?"

"Even better," answered Germaine, feeling sure she could trust her old friend, and even feeling a bit ashamed that she hadn't revealed everything to him when she was at his house. "We are pretty sure we have discovered his true identity."

Germaine and Helen related their findings to Chauncey. They told him how Germaine found the locket, what Edward Bartlett and Federicka Kroch told her about the monogram, the old journals of Miss Rose, the hidden compartment in Germaine's house, the letters, and finally they showed him the photographs of Lorenzo Santini and Aubrey Bowles III and let him compare them with the newspaper engravings of the Swarthy Swiper.

"I'd know that face anywhere," Chauncey whispered as he looked at the old newspaper illustrations. "A.B. Three is the spitting image of his father and grandfather."

"I believe he was responsible for all those thefts and that he put it about that Lorenzo Santini was a thief in order to throw the suspicions away from himself. I think he chose to use the initials L.S. as a way to further lead people to believe Lorenzo was the Swiper," Germaine said, seriously.

"The rounder!" exclaimed Chauncey. "Imagine, casting suspicion on his wife's beloved sister's husband to hide his own dastardly deeds. Poor Lucetta!"

The friends agreed that their next step was to discover why Colonel Aubrey Bowles had committed the crimes.

"Germaine," Helen said, looking over at her friend. "You're awfully quiet. What's on your mind?"

"I was just thinking about that orphanage that the first Aubrey Bowles founded in Boston. It doesn't seem to be in keeping with his character to be stealing from lonely widows one moment and constructing an orphanage the next," she answered.

"Aren't you the one always telling me that no one is all bad or all good?" asked Chauncey.

"I am, indeed. And I'm sure Aubrey had many admirable qualities. I'd just like to know a bit more about this orphanage," Germaine replied.

"Do you think he was a Robin Hood character? Stealing from the rich to fund an orphanage for the poor?" Helen asked.

"I don't know," Germaine replied. "But if he was, why drag Lorenzo Santini's name through the mud?"

"Could it have been a coincidence that he came up with names that had the initials L.S.?" Helen asked, not really believing that was possible.

"Hardly," said Germaine. "He was whispering behind Lorenzo's back that he was a jewel thief. There's no coincidence here."

"Well the Bowles kept everything with any of their names on it," said Chauncey, as the trio discussed how best to get to the bottom of the mystery. "A.B. Three's father, whom we'll call A.B. Two, was as convinced of his own greatness as the son is. Number Two kept all the family paperwork he could get his hands on. It's stored in a bunch of metal file cabinets in their refinished basement. Their carpeted refinished basement," he rolled his eyes at this design choice. "I could just tell Number Three that I need to look something up and I'm sure he'd let me down there."

"But didn't A.B. Three give you everything you needed from their end for your research?" asked Helen.

"More than enough," answered Chauncey. "But he doesn't know that. He really doesn't care about the family history; that was his father's thing. What this one cares about is just looking like he's got some family history and gravitas."

"I'll bet if he knew the real history of his family he might change his tune," Germaine said. "He may want an unmarked grave, never mind a giant gauche mausoleum when he learns about his grandfather."

"I'll call him this afternoon," Chauncey said in a conspiratorial tone, "and see if I can spend a few hours in the basement. Please note the supreme sacrifice I am making in the pursuit of truth, justice, and historical accuracy – a carpeted basement!"

The girls laughed so heartily that a few of the older patrons in the museum turned around to shush them. Chastened, they quietly rewound the microfilm they had been using and gathered up the photos and locket. Germaine put the precious goods in her case and Helen returned the library materials to their proper shelves. The friends decided to have lunch before they did any more sleuthing. Germaine knew that Mrs. White would be happy to make lunch for guests, so she invited her two chums over for something to eat before they continued their work.

Mrs. White was only too happy to oblige; her one request was that Germaine go outside and pick some ramps and chives from the garden. Surprised that there might be anything edible back there, the hostess leapt at the chance to be of help to her faithful housekeeper and to check on the progress that Andrew McGrath was making in the old garden.

Andrew showed the three friends what he had accomplished to date. The transformation was nearly complete, and Germaine smiled admiringly as she saw how different the space looked. Where there were once tangles of brambles, weeds, and unidentifiable vegetation there were now orderly beds of flowers, herbs and vegetables. Andrew had followed the original plans to the letter and was recreating a thriving Victorian garden single-handedly.

"Heavens!" Germaine exclaimed as the beaming Andrew helped her gather up the greens requested by Mrs. White. "I can hardly believe this is the same space, Andrew. I have been so busy that I haven't even poked my head out to look at your progress. It's magnificent!"

Andrew McGrath beamed even more broadly. He showed Helen and Chauncey around as Germaine brought the food into Mrs. White, who agreed with Germaine that Andrew had done a tremendous job in a very short time. "I don't much like that Littleton boy, though," said Mrs. White.

"Who?" asked Germaine.

"Pugsy Littleton. He comes here and pesters Andrew McGrath. Andrew's a good lad, and a very hard worker, and that Pugsy comes by and just lies about. He could at least give a hand, but he's always been an idle boy. Sometimes he disappears for a while, off fishing in the river, I'd wager, but then he pops up again and asks Andrew lots of questions. I can't hear what they're talking about, but I just get a bad feeling from that one." Mrs. White had seen her share of all sorts of people in her life, and Germaine trusted her evaluation of the boy, but she truly did believe no one was all bad or all good, especially a young person. She hoped that Andrew would be a good influence on the Littleton boy, and she made a mental note to keep better track of the goings on in the garden and to introduce herself to Pugsy Littleton if she saw him out there.

Eventually, the three friends sat down in the dining room. The table was laid with a floral Wedgewood china that was perfectly suited to the late spring meal. Delicate crystal tumblers were at the right of each place setting, and the everyday silver with its simple M monogram was laid upon the white cotton napkins. Mrs. White had prepared a fluffy quiche with early peas and topped with chives, simple boiled new potatoes, and a crisp and lightly dressed salad of ramps and other greens. As always, she served just the right quantity for the people present. The chums enjoyed a pitcher of cool water with delicate lemon slices with their meal. As they enjoyed luncheon, they discussed the case and marveled at the twists and turns since the discovery of the locket.

"I had no idea these G. Taylor Wood houses had secret compartments and the like," Chauncey said, as Helen revealed where and how they had found the sisters' old correspondence. "Do you think the jewels are hidden somewhere in the house? Perhaps there's another secret hiding place that you don't know anything about," he said tantalizingly.

"I have wondered the same thing," Germaine answered thoughtfully after she dabbed her lips with her napkin. "Lucetta and Aubrey lived in this house for some time, and he could have hidden the jewels here. They moved in soon after their marriage to take care of Lyman Sheppard, but then they moved to Boston after Lyman died and Philippa and Lorenzo moved back to the house to raise Rose."

"I bet Colonel Bowles was too embarrassed to live under the same roof as the man he'd wrongfully slandered," said

Helen, who like Chauncey, had a thoroughly low opinion of the late Colonel Aubrey Bowles.

"But then again, Aubrey might have been frightened that Philippa would find the jewels and would discover that he was the Swarthy Swiper all along. It would have been very dangerous to leave them here, a house where the two sisters presumably knew all the nooks and crannies," Germaine countered.

"Germaine," Helen asked her friend, "Why do you think Philippa and Lucetta hid their letters?"

"I don't think it was Philippa and Lucetta who hid them," Germaine said with an enigmatic smile, "and if my hunch is right, the letters and the locket were left just where they were in order to point someone in the direction of the jewels."

Just as Chauncey and Helen were about to grill their clever friend for more details, there was a very loud crash from beneath the dining room's bay window.

Chapter Fourteen: "Call the police!"

The three leapt up and ran to the bay window. Helen and Germaine knelt on the tailored velvet cushions of the window seat and peered into the yard below as Chauncey pulled aside one of the hand-embroidered Italian lace panels. As the three friends looked down, they saw a young boy hopping about on one leg while holding his scraped knee with both hands and yelping "aaaaaaooooowwww!"

Germaine rushed outside to help the boy, and her friends were close behind. "Are you alright?" she asked with sincere concern. "Chauncey, please ask Mrs. White for the first aid kit. It's in the pantry."

As Chauncey went to fetch the kit, Germaine and Helen tried to comfort the boy. He was terribly frightened that he had been caught eavesdropping, but he quickly realized that they didn't know he'd climbed up the lattice beside the window and was hanging on their words when he'd fallen to the ground. He shrewdly calculated how best to take advantage of the situation.

"I was just coming up the walk to see if I could help my friend Andy McGrath with his gardening chores and I tripped," Pugsy choked out between fake sobs. He knew ladies didn't like to see people cry.

"Oh dear," said Germaine and Helen in unison as they looked in vain to see what he might have tripped over. "Well, it doesn't look too serious," Helen said tentatively.

"Can you straighten your knee out and try to walk?" asked Germaine, who had quickly realized that the boy was exaggerating his injuries. She rightly deduced that this was the unlikeable Pugsy Littleton that Mrs. White had described, but she was determined to see the good in him.

Chauncey came out with a little tin decorated with a red cross that contained ointments and bandages. He cleaned the boy's knee with alcohol, and as Pugsy winced in real pain, Germaine straightened up and noticed that the trellis had pulled away from the house ever so slightly. She walked over to inspect it and saw dirty little fingerprints at window height. As her eyes moved toward the window, she saw Mrs. White standing at it with her arms crossed and one eyebrow raised.

"Pugsy," Germaine began sternly, "why were you listening at the window?"

Chauncey dropped the first aid kit and it rattled to the ground. Helen dropped her jaw, and the two looked from Germaine to Pugsy to see what this boy, upon whom they'd never before set eyes, would say to that surprising accusation. Pugsy began to stammer something and looked from Germaine to Chauncey to Helen with panicked eyes. Finally, he clambered to his feet and ran away.

"Heavens!" exclaimed Helen. "How did you know that boy's name?" she asked.

"And how did you know he was eavesdropping on us?" Chauncey continued.

Germaine explained everything, and as she finished, Mrs. White opened the screen of the window to lean out and give some advice. "That boy is no good. If you ask me, he's looking to rob you. He heard you talking about hidden jewels and he's aiming to break in and take them. You should ban him from the property, Germaine. Call the police and tell them to be on the lookout for him, or there will be more trouble down the line."

"Oh, Mrs. White," Germaine answered gently, grateful for her faithful housekeeper's concern, "I think we'll be okay. He's only a child, after all. I would hate for him to be involved with the police at such a young age."

"Better they get him now and lock him up before he does real damage is what I say," said Mrs. White. "And five will get you ten he was the one digging holes in the garden looking for treasure."

Andrew McGrath had come from the garden to see what all the commotion was about. When Mrs. White filled him in on the details, Andrew's face turned a deep shade of red and he looked at his shoes.

"Gee, Mrs. White, Miss Germaine..." he said quietly. "I'm sorry I ever told Pugsy that I was working for you. I will send him away if he comes back here."

"It's not your fault, Andrew," Germaine said kindly. "You were just trying to encourage young Mr. Littleton to get an honest job."

"Young Mr. Littleton, indeed," scoffed Mrs. White. "If I see him on your property again, I'm calling the police, Germaine," and as she said this, she looked witheringly at Andrew McGrath.

Luckily for Andrew, he missed the wrath of Mrs. White's gaze, because he was fishing about in his pocket when it was directed at him.

"I wanted to show you this," he said, opening his palm up towards Germaine. "I think it's an Indian arrowhead!"

Germaine, Chauncey, and Helen all leaned forward to get a better look at the object.

"Niantic jasper," Chauncey said almost at once. Helen scraped off some of the dirt from the object and revealed a mustard yellow color.

"I concur," she concurred, "500 A.D."

"Gosh!" Andrew gazed at the tiny piece of stone in his hand. "How do you know all that?"

"Chauncey and Helen both studied the history of the native people of this region when they were at Elmhurst," Germaine explained.

"We have beginner courses at the Historical Society," Helen said. "I believe Germaine picked up a schedule of classes for you."

"Colonial silver one day, Indian arrowheads the next," Germaine laughed. "You never know what this old garden of mine will turn up."

"There's a bunch of pottery pieces, too," Andrew added. "I put them in a pile near the shed."

"Ah, but a bunch of old pottery doesn't hold a candle to an actual Indian arrowhead, eh Andrew?" said Chauncey, giving the boy a nudge.

"No, sir," said Andrew earnestly.

"Maybe you'll find a tomahawk, too," Chauncey said, remembering the pleasure he had as a boy in playing cowboys and Indians and hunting for buried Indian treasure. Andrew's eyes grew wide at the thought of finding a tomahawk in Germaine Moreau's garden.

"I'll tell you what, Andrew," Germaine said, rolling her eyes at Helen in response to the boys' talk of native artifacts.

"You keep that arrowhead. I'll let you use my special archeological brush to clean it off."

"Really? Oh gosh, thank you, Miss Germaine!" Andrew McGrath could hardly believe his luck.

"Yellow jasper is said to bring strength to those who carry it," Germaine said seriously. "So if Pugsy Littleton comes around here and you see him, I want you to be strong enough to send him away. The arrowhead will help you find the strength."

"Yes, Miss Germaine. Oh, thank you!" Andrew said, as Helen and Chauncey winked at each other, appreciating the cleverness of Germaine's story.

"Just don't shoot it at him," Chauncey added with a smile

The young friends agreed that they would all keep a special eye out for him, but were confident they could handle any trouble that the ten year old Littleton boy might send their way.

"Well come and have some desert, then," Mrs. White said before closing the window.

Helen and Chauncey happily returned inside, but Germaine spent a few minutes chatting with Andrew in the garden before rejoining her friends. As the others happily chatted over the exquisite lemon curd squares Mrs. White had prepared, Germaine sat quietly, absorbed in her own thoughts.

Her friends left after lunch and Germaine returned to the sisters' letters. She had been reading them over for some time when the telephone rang.

"Germaine!" Chauncey whispered loudly over the telephone. "Aubrey One had terrible gambling debts. He owed money to every casino on the East Coast and several in Europe." Chauncey had taken seven boxes of papers from the Bowles' family's basement and brought them home with him. As his headquarters – the dining room – was already covered in papers related to other projects he was working on, he brought the boxes up to the games room and had sorted the papers into piles on the intricately carved Edwardian snooker table. He had gingerly placed the papers that detailed Colonel Aubrey Bowles' gambling debts on the green baize of the billiards table, and then dialed his friend to relate what he'd found.

"Are you in their house now?" asked Germaine in a low tone to match Chauncey's.

"No, I'm in my house, up in the games room."

"Why are we whispering?" asked Germaine, confused.

"I'm not sure. But I'll stop now." Chauncey said. He went on, in a normal voice, "I guess this explains why he stole the jewels. He must have sold them to pay off his debts. There are several records of huge debts having been suddenly paid off, after Bowles received lots of threatening letters about the debt."

"Anything about an orphanage?" Germaine asked.

"What do you think?" Chauncey replied derisively.

"I would like to give Aubrey Bowles the benefit of the doubt until proven otherwise," she said.

"That's because you're such a good egg, Germaine," Chauncey said admiring his friend's compassion. "There was no orphanage. Aubrey Bowles the first was a gambler, a liar, a thief, and a slanderer."

"Poor Lucetta," sighed Germaine. "I wonder if she knew?" she went on, her voice trailing off.

"Why don't you and Helen come over here so we can look at this stuff together. You might see something I've missed. And bring the letters. Maybe if we look at the dates of all the documents, we can piece together a timeline of the thefts and Lorenzo Santini's travels. The least we can do is set the record straight and clear Santini's name," Chauncey said, chivalrously.

"That's a grand idea. I'll collect Helen and the letters and we'll be there soon. That will allow plenty of time for the lemonade you'll make for us to get nice and cold!" Germaine said with a smile.

"Okay, fine," answered Chauncey, "but you have to bring one of Mrs. White's pies with you." Mrs. White's pies were a particular favorite in the Fetterson household. Fortunately, Mrs. White had left a pecan one to cool before she'd left for the day. Germaine knew Chauncey would enjoy it.

As Germaine hung up the phone, she thought of something else she wanted to bring to Chauncey Fetterson's house. She ran up to the attic to gather all of Miss Rose's diaries. She hoped that re-reading them with the knowledge she now had about the Sheppard family might prove enlightening. As she stepped on the mechanism that unlocked the secret door, Germaine's head was full of thoughts about the locket, the key, the Swarthy Swiper, the letters, and the sisters, so she didn't notice that there was someone lurking about in the attic. As soon as she stepped into the secret room, the door swung closed behind her with a thud. She heard something being dragged across the floor and then propped up against the secret door. Someone had locked her in and blocked any chance she had of pushing the door open from inside!

Chapter Fifteen: Trapped!

"Hey!" she yelled. "Who's there? Why have you locked me in here? This is my house!" There was no response. As her eyes adjusted to the dim light, she could tell that someone had riffled through all of Miss Rose's diaries and other belongings. The books were scattered on the floor and the old shoeboxes were all upended. She yelled again, but heard footsteps running down the attic stairs, so she gave up. She had picked up the flashlight on her way into the attic, and she felt around for it on the floor. The light had been dim when she had used it a few days earlier, but she hoped it still had enough power to help her find a way out. She trained the weak beam on the walls and floors of the hidden room and began a methodic search for a twin of the floor mechanism that would open the door from the inside. She started in one corner and made her way carefully, inch by inch, across the floor in a grid pattern. She knew that this was the most efficient way to find a release button if one existed. The light dimmed and flickered. "Oh why didn't I change the batteries when I saw how weak they were," Germaine chastised herself.

She sat down and removed the batteries, gave each one a good shake, and put them back in the flashlight in reverse order. This strengthened the light and she continued on her examination of the space. "There must be a way out of here," she thought. Several times, she found nails sticking out of the wall or lumps on the floor that she was sure would open the door. But not one of them did. With nothing else to do, and not the type of person to sit around idly if there was something that could be done, she straightened the old diaries into piles. She couldn't see well enough to read them, so she couldn't put them back into chronological order, but at least she was able to tidy things up. The flashlight went out entirely as she was completing this task. She squinted and felt around for the other objects on the floor and placed them carefully into the shoeboxes. Germaine made a mental note to include some sort of an escape route if she ever decided to build a hidden room.

"Hellooooo!" she called out, and received no response. Suddenly the silence of the attic was broken by the muted and distant ring of the telephone. Germaine was sure it was Chauncey calling to see why she and Helen hadn't arrived yet. She knew it had probably been more than an hour since she told Chauncey that she would arrive at his house. "They'll come here eventually," she reasoned, "and when I hear them in the house, I'll call out and they'll get me out of here."

Germaine slunk down in a corner of the secret room with resignation. She hoped her friends would be quick in coming to look for her. "Who on earth would have locked me in this room? And why?" Germaine couldn't imagine why anyone would want to play such a trick on her. It wasn't like Helen to do such a thing, and while Chauncey might have been capable of a practical joke, she knew he was at his house. "Besides," she said out loud, "Chauncey would have laughed and let me out after a few minutes."

Germaine thought about how mean and childish practical jokes were, and then the image of Pugsy Littleton flashed into her mind. She gave out a startled gasp. "Pugsy is small enough to have fit behind those boxes in the corner," she told herself. "Perhaps he was trying to punish me for embarrassing him when I caught him snooping at lunch." But Germaine found it difficult to believe that the young boy would be so audacious as to break in to her house and lie in wait for her. "And how would he have even known this room existed?" she mused. She began to doubt whether the door was pushed shut after all. "What if it just sort of closed on its own? And maybe I didn't really hear footsteps… maybe it was just creaking attic noises," she thought, giving the boy the benefit of the doubt.

As Germaine sat in the close, windowless space, she began to get drowsy, and she eventually put her head down and fell asleep, with the faint trill of the ringing telephone sounding frequently in the distance. "If worst comes to worst," she thought before surrendering to sleep, "Mrs. White will come and find me when she gets here tomorrow."

*   *   *

"Germaine! Germaine! Can you hear me?" Germaine slowly blinked her eyes open only to slam them shut again in the glare of a flashlight that was working as it was designed to do.

"I'm fine, Edward, thank you, and how are you?" she asked, with automatic politeness.

"Oh Germaine, we were so worried about you!" this was from Helen, who along with Edward Bartlett and Chauncey Fetterson was standing in the small secret room. Chauncey and Helen helped Germaine up, while Edward went off to fetch a damp facecloth and a glass of water. He quickly returned with both, which restored the young woman.

"What happened?" the newly arrived trio said in unison. Germaine told them she thought it was a draft that had caused the door to shut behind her, hoping to spare Pugsy Littleton's reputation since she had no proof of her suspicion.

"Draft indeed," snorted Edward Bartlett indignantly. "Your house has been ransacked. Someone deliberately locked you in this room. Thank heavens your friends had sense enough to come looking for you, or who knows how long you would have been here."

"Ransacked?" exclaimed Germaine, standing up.

"You'd better see for yourself," Helen said, gently. The friends led Germaine downstairs and she inspected each room, which had, indeed, been ransacked. In her bedroom, the bureau drawers had all been removed and there were clothes strewn everywhere. The music room was covered in sheet music, all of it unsheathed and scattered. The library was a total disaster with shelves upended, books tossed carelessly about, and files emptied.

"Oh dear," sighed Germaine after seeing the rooms on the top floor of her house. Her friends thought that Germaine was upset at the condition of her home. Which she was, but she also noticed that none of the drawers or shelves that were over five feet from the ground had been disturbed. "Pugsy," she concluded, silently.

Germaine regained her strength immediately, and insisted on making tea for everyone. The small group sat around a simple walnut table in the kitchen. Germaine tidied things up in the kitchen as the tea brewed, and sliced up the pecan pie that she had intended to bring to Chauncey Fetterson's house. Edward Bartlett chuckled when she gave him a piece. "Leave it to you, Germaine, to be able to serve three unexpected guests pecan pie and tea right after your house has been broken into and you've been locked in a secret room."

"Three unexpected rescuers," Germaine corrected the kindly old jeweler, as she finished putting the kitchen in order. "There," she said, sitting down to join the others, "at least one room is back to normal.

"But Edward," she continued, "you *are* unexpected. Did Chauncey and Helen phone you? How long was I locked up there?" she wondered.

"No dear, no one called me," explained Edward Bartlett. "I came here to see you."

"Oh, of course. You've just come back from New York. I had nearly forgotten that you said you would stop by after your trip. You said on the phone you had something to show me," Germaine said, feeling much better as the tea warmed her up.

"It's about the locket and the Santini jewels," Edward said, placing a large envelope on the kitchen table.

"The locket!" Germaine dropped her fork and rushed upstairs to the library, which was still in terrible disarray. It seemed that the sisters' letters were still there, although completely out of order, and she found the photographs of the Sheppards, Santinis, and Bowles' that she had been collecting. Some of the photos were bent and torn from their rough handling. At last, she spotted the brocade pouch that she'd sewn for the locket, tossed near the door. She feared the worst when she couldn't see the outline of the locket in the fabric. She picked it up and fears were confirmed. The pouch was empty.

Chapter Sixteen: Gone!

The others had waited in the kitchen, and were discussing the happenings of the last few days.

"This is certainly becoming a strange mystery," Helen said. "I am shocked that someone would lock Germaine into a room in her own house."

"A hidden room, at that," Chauncey added, gravely. "I think Mrs. White is right. We should call the police. Especially if something has been stolen."

"In the old days, respectable ladies only wished to see their names in the paper –" Edward began, and was interrupted by Chauncey and Helen joining him to complete the sentence, "— for weddings and deaths," the trio chanted.

"And now things have changed," Edward said, "but I don't think Germaine's name would have appeared in the newspaper if she did call the police about this break in. Although I can see that she might not like the neighbors to worry that there's a cat burglar on the loose, assuming this was a targeted break in."

"That's a good point, Edward," Helen said thoughtfully. "But what if there is a burglar on the loose breaking into houses here in Springdale. Surely people need to know if this is one in a string of robberies."

"I have a feeling this was not random at all," Edward said.

"And I have a feeling that if anyone can figure it out without the police, Germaine Moreau can," Chauncey said with a smile.

"I think your faith in me will prove well-placed," Germaine said with determination as she entered the kitchen."

"Come on, Chauncey," she said as she searched for the keys to her car. "You and I have to pay a visit to someone." Everyone else looked confused, but Germaine was quite confident of where the locket was and how to get it back.

"Germaine, dear, where on earth are you going at this late hour?" Edward asked.

"Are you sure you're in a condition to drive?" Helen added.

"I got quite a nice little nap while I was locked in that room," Germaine answered, "and I think I will be able to solve several mysteries with one trip."

"I hate to impose on my friends, but would you two stay here?" she asked of Helen and Edward, who both nodded without hesitation. "If we aren't back within the hour, call the police and tell them to go to this address," Germaine said, handing a piece of ivory stationery to Edward. "Ask for Sergeant Howard." Mr. Howard was from an old Springdale family and Germaine was sure of his competence and discretion.

Germaine and Chauncey were off in a flash, and Edward and Helen just looked at each other in wonder. As Germaine and Chauncey drove off to a very poor section of Springdale, Edward explained to Helen the reason for his visit. There had been something vaguely familiar about the locket that Germaine had shown him, and it had been nagging at him since he'd seen it. One night, it came to him in his sleep – the locket had been reported as stolen by Philippa Santini, and the Swarthy Swiper was the suspect. Although best known for his rash crimes in New York, Philadelphia, and Boston, the Swiper had struck several times in Springdale. Edward looked up the insurance records and found that the locket Germaine found in the garden had been reported as stolen from this very house. Helen told Edward what the young people had learned about the Swarthy Swiper's identity.

"Will wonders never cease?" asked Edward when he learned that Colonel Aubrey Bowles was the likely culprit. "They're a bad lot, those Bowles men. I don't know why I'm surprised. But to stoop to slander, well, that's just ungentlemanly, even for a Bowles," he concluded.

Helen led the elderly man upstairs to the library. She wanted to show Mr. Bartlett the photographs and the newspaper engravings that the girls had gathered. She thought Germaine wouldn't mind if she tidied things up in the room, since she knew where most of the papers and books belonged. Helen cleared the jumbled papers off Germaine's elegant kidney-shaped desk and turned on a lamp so that the older man could better see. As he pored over the photographs and illustrations, Helen replaced the desk and cabinet drawers that had been strewn about the room. She re-organized all the paperwork as best she could and managed to put the library back into some sort of order, but she quickly realized that many of the newspaper clippings had vanished.

As Helen tidied and Edward looked at the documents the young people had collected, Chauncey was looking out the window of Germaine's car, surprised at the route she was following.

"I didn't even know some of these streets existed, Germaine," he said with wonder. "Where are we?"

"This is where Mrs. White and her husband lived when they first came to Springdale," Germaine explained. "Sometimes my folks would pick her up for work and I would tag along. She lives in a much nicer section near the park now, but they were quite poor when they first arrived here."

"Well, if we're not visiting the White's ancestral home, what on earth are we doing here?" Chauncey asked.

"Getting the locket back and teaching a young boy a lesson," Germaine answered seriously as she got out of her car and knocked on the door of a ramshackle three-family house.

Stray cats were roaming through the yards and there were garbage cans with no lids near the door.

"And who might you be looking for at this hour of the night?" asked the woman who answered the door.

"Good evening, I'm looking for Pugsy Littleton," Germaine answered, the picture of politeness.

"Figures," the woman said. "Second floor, rear."

Germaine thanked the woman for the information as she and her friend climbed the stairs. "Can you believe they split these into even more apartments?" Chauncey asked. "They're tiny to begin with."

"I'll bet Pugsy lives in small and crowded quarters," Germaine responded.

"Well that's no excuse for stealing and locking you in a room," Chauncey sniffed.

"Of course it's not an excuse, but if a boy is surrounded by such squalor all day, he may have dreams of a better life, and not know any better way to achieve that life than through crime," Germaine said with compassion.

"And what's Aubrey Bowles, the Swarthy Swiper's excuse? He certainly didn't live in squalor," Chauncey said.

"I don't think there is any excuse for criminal behavior, rich or poor," Germaine explained as they reached the grimy door to the Littleton apartment, "but I do think that Pugsy's crime is more understandable than Aubrey's." Germaine checked her watch and knocked at the door.

A man appeared at the door in an undershirt and work pants. He had a can of beer in one hand.

"What?" he said by way of greeting. "Are you from the school?"

"Good evening," Germaine said, extending her hand. "My name is Germaine Moreau, and I am here to speak with Pugsy."

"Chauncey Fetterson," Chauncey said, reluctantly following Germaine's lead and shaking the man's free hand.

"What did the little monster do this time?" the man asked, putting down the can of beer. "Pugsy!" he yelled, "Get over here, *now!*"

As Pugsy slunk into view, his father lifted his hand menacingly, as if to strike the boy. Germaine quickly moved between them and asked if she could speak with Pugsy privately. Mr. Littleton grunted his consent and motioned towards the kitchen. As Germaine and Pugsy walked into the kitchen, the father made his way towards a room that the Littletons appeared to use as a sitting and dining room. A radio perched on a lopsided table was broadcasting a sporting match of some sort. Chauncey stood in the hallway, unsure of whether to follow Germaine, follow Mr. Littleton, or just stay where he was.

"You may as well come and sit here," the father said, appreciating Chauncey's uncertainty. "We're up two," he said, nodding towards the radio.

Chauncey nodded and pretended to be engaged by the game, profoundly relieved that he wouldn't be forced to make small talk with Pugsy's father.

As the men sat listening to the radio, Germaine sat Pugsy down at the kitchen table. "Why do you think I'm here?" she asked him, sternly.

"I dunno," he shrugged, refusing to meet her gaze.

"Pugsy." Germaine just needed to say the boy's name in the right tone of voice before he started squirming in his seat.

"Oh, alright. I'm sorry," he said, quite unconvincingly. "I took the locket, and I locked you in that room. I overheard you and the other lady talking about the room and the letters and the locket, and I took it," Pugsy said, sounding more like he was boasting about his shameful escapade than regretting it.

"Pugsy, it's wrong to steal, it's wrong to eavesdrop, and it's wrong to lock someone in a room," Germaine said, seriously. "Why did you do such bad things?"

"You're already rich. You don't need that locket. And I knew you'd get out of the room. Look, here you are, so you weren't locked in that long," his defiant attitude continued.

"Pugsy, it doesn't matter how rich one person is or how poor another person is. It is never right to steal," Germaine sat and looked steadily at Pugsy. After a few moments in Germaine's steady gaze, Pugsy eventually uncrossed his arms and looked Germaine in the eye.

"I'm sorry Miss Germaine," he finally said, quietly and sincerely. He pulled the locket out of his pocket and put it on the table. "My father's going to kill me."

"I'm not going to tell your father what you did, and I'm not going to tell the police either, at least not right now. You have a lot of creative energy and extra time on your hands. If you want more from life than what you have now, you have to go out and work for it, not steal for it. If you straighten out and find a job, I will not go to the police about this incident."

"But I'm too young to work," Pugsy said, reminding Germaine of child labor laws.

"You're not too young to deliver newspapers or clean up the sidewalks for a shop owner. You can go down to the Gazette office and get a newspaper delivery route tomorrow, or you can ask some of the shopkeepers downtown if you can help them clean up. But if I catch you loafing about and not working, just complaining, I will contact the police, and you could go to jail. Do you understand?"

Pugsy indicated that he did understand, and the two walked out of the kitchen and into the room where the men were.

"What did he do this time?" Mr. Littleton said, only half-listening to the response, as there was an especially detailed play on the radio.

"Pugsy dug some holes in my garden," Germaine said, observing Pugsy out of the corner of her eye, and he reacted with great surprise that she knew he was also responsible for that misdeed. "But he has agreed to make amends. I hope this will be the end of the story."

Chauncey was utterly confused, but he simply stood up and shook Mr. Littleton's hand and gave Pugsy what he hoped was a withering look. The two returned to Germaine's car, and Germaine related the story to Chauncey.

"Do you think he'll straighten out and get a job?" Chauncey asked as they neared the Sheppard house.

"I guess we'll have to wait and see," Germaine said. "But I do hope the answer will be yes."

*   *   *

Moments after Helen replaced the contents in the final desk drawer, she and Edward heard the front door open. Worried at first that the burglars had returned, both Helen and Edward sighed with relief when they heard Germaine call out "I've got the locket back!"

Germaine and Chauncey made their way upstairs and were both impressed at how tidy the library was after the ransacking.

"It's been less than three-quarters of an hour," Helen said, "how on earth did you find the locket so quickly?"

"Germaine made me promise not to mention anything about how we recovered the locket," Chauncey said, clearly regretting the oath he'd made to his friend as he straightened his necktie uncomfortably. "But you could probably pry it out of me in exchange for that sterling and amber paperweight," he said to Edward Bartlett, not entirely joking.

In their college days, Germaine frequently brought one or both of her young chums to visit her dear old friend in his jewelry shop. Chauncey had an impressive collection of antique paperweights, which came in quite useful in securing the many piles of papers he had around his house, and he had coveted the unusual specimen in Bartlett's Family Jewels at first sight.

"What's important is *that* you got it back, not *how* you got it back," Edward said, kindly. "I'll ask no questions, and I'll keep my paperweight, thank you very much. Now, as to the reason for my visit…"

Chapter Seventeen: The woman in the veil

Edward Bartlett told the young people that ever since Germaine visited him and showed him the locket, he had been thinking about the woman in the veil who had come into the shop when he was just a young boy. One night while he was in New York, he dreamed about the exquisite chest of jewels that the woman had brought to show Edward's father, and in his dream, the key in Germaine's locket opened that chest. He decided to look through all the old records, and he found a piece of paper that caused the memory of that day to come rushing back to him. He had discovered who the woman in the veil was, he knew to whom the locket belonged, and he wanted to come and show Germaine everything.

"It was a very sunny afternoon, that day nearly sixty years ago when the elegant woman dressed all in black came into the shop. She was not an old woman, in fact she was surely younger than I am now, but she carried herself as if she had borne a lifetime of troubles. When mother and father discussed her visit at the dinner table that night, they surmised she was a widow," he began.

"You mean to say she didn't give her name," Chauncey asked, hanging on Edward's every word.

"Not that day. When she first entered the shop, the woman in the veil placed a small chest on the counter. It shone with the reflected light of the sun, and my father was taken aback by the beauty of the object. I remember wanting to run over and touch it, but I knew I oughtn't, so I just stood there.

"'Would you please draw the shades and lock the door, Mr. Bartlett,' she asked in a very refined voice, 'My inquiry is of a most delicate nature.'

"My father obliged, and motioned for me to go sit at the repair bench in the rear of the shop. The woman drew a tiny gold key from her pocket, and with her elegant gloved hand turned the key in the lock. The chest, which was constructed of the finest gold and inlaid with pearls and lapis lazuli opened silently. One by one, the woman extracted exquisite pieces of antique jewelry: opal earrings that quivered on fine wires, strand after strand of luminous natural pearls, cuffed bracelets encrusted with stones, and one of the biggest canary diamond rings I have ever seen," Edward told the story almost as if in a trance of memory, and the young people all sat on the edge of their seats, transfixed by the tale.

"The woman laid the final piece on the black velvet cloth my father had provided. It was a large gold locket. It was your locket, Germaine. Well, the one you found. I remember it as clear as day now, even though I was probably only five or six at the time."

"Go on," Germaine urged her friend, breathlessly.

"I had been sitting at the repair bench, but I could see each piece she laid on the counter. I didn't make a sound, and perhaps father forgot I was there. These jewels would make you forget anything. As the woman closed the small chest and the top clicked into place, I strained to get a better look at the chest. The woman noticed this sudden movement and asked father if the two of them could discuss her situation privately. Of course my father obliged and sent me away."

"Oh Mr. Bartlett," Helen said wistfully, "how I wish you'd been able to hear their conversation!"

"I did," he answered with a smile.

"How?" Helen and Chauncey asked in unison.

"If I know Edward," Germaine said, winking at her old friend, "he sat just outside the door so that he could obey his father and satisfy his curiosity at the same time."

"You do know Edward, dear," said Edward. "That's just what I did. And it has all come back to me vividly. I can remember their conversation as if it happened yesterday."

"'Mr. Bartlett,' the woman began, addressing my father. 'I must request your discretion and confidentiality before I tell you what has brought me here today.'

"'Certainly, madam,' said father, probably thinking the young widow had fallen on hard times and wished to sell some family heirlooms.

"'Your family has been in the jewelry business for a long time, and has a spotless reputation,' she went on. Father thanked her for the kind words.

"'I was given these jewels by my mother. I have reason to believe that they were stolen from her late sister, my aunt. If that is the case, I would like to return them to my cousin, who would be the rightful heir to them. I want them returned anonymously. She is to have no knowledge of how the jewels were taken from her mother or how they were returned to her. But first, I must ascertain that they are indeed her late mother's jewels and not someone else's property.'"

Germaine, Helen, and Chauncey sat in rapt silence, barely breathing as they waited to hear what happened next. Edward Bartlett was silent, too.

Finally, Chauncey couldn't take the suspense. "Then what happened?" he urged; knowing that Edward liked to take his time and build up a gripping story, but unable to restrain himself from asking for more.

"Then," Edward went on, looking from listener to listener and finally settling his gaze on Chauncey. "Then," he repeated, "mother came down the stairs and boxed my ears for listening in on a private conversation. I got a good spanking and went to bed with no dinner."

"Maybe if Pugsy had gotten a good spanking when he was listening in on a private conversation, he'd straighten out, too," Chauncey said.

Germaine ignored this comment and turned to Edward. "So you have no idea who the woman was?" she asked, half expecting Edward to have said that the sisters and cousins in the story were the Sheppard daughters and their offspring.

"I didn't until just a few days ago. I learned my lesson about eavesdropping and I didn't dare ask my folks about the mysterious woman or the beautiful jewels. I thought about those jewels and that chest now and again throughout the years. But it had been ages since it had popped into my mind until you walked into the shop with that locket, Germaine.

"As I said, something kept gnawing at me, and I looked up the old records. The woman in the veil was Viola Bowles, daughter of Colonel Aubrey Bowles and Lucetta Sheppard Bowles. Most of the jewels in the chest, and the chest itself, had indeed belonged to Lucetta's sister, Philippa Santini, but some of them had been reported stolen right around the turn of the century."

"How do you know all this?" Chauncey asked.

"Insurance records," Helen responded. "An insurance case against missing items with a certain value does not close for fifty years."

Everyone looked at Helen with amazement.

"Quite right, child," said Edward Bartlett, admiringly, "but how on earth did you know that?"

"I am a research librarian," she responded with a proud smile, "we know just about all there is to know about records."

"Well, as may be old news to Helen here," Edward continued, "there were insurance claims against some of the jewels. Interestingly, *not* against the Santini items, save one."

"Philippa wouldn't have wanted to launch an investigation that might have harmed her sister," Germaine said quietly.

"Quite right," Edward said. "You seem to have a good grasp of Philippa's character."

"Helen and I have been reading over their old correspondence," Germaine explained.

"I see that," Edward responded. "Helen and I tidied things up in here, and she showed me a few of them. But even without those letters as proof," he said. "I know full well that the jewels that were not reported as stolen were indeed Philippa's."

Chapter Eighteen: Revelations

"How!?" the three friends said as one.

"Wait, Edward," Germaine interrupted. "You said none of the Santini jewels was reported stolen, *save one*. Which one was that?"

"The locket," Edward said, and with a flourish, pulled an old and yellowing paper from the envelope he'd brought with him.

"I went to New York to find the original insurance records," he said, pulling page after page from the envelope. "It turns out, Philippa filed an insurance claim when her beloved golden locket was stolen, and that triggered a full investigation into her jewelry holdings."

"Why would she just file one claim if she'd had many things stolen?" Helen asked.

"The locket was special to her," Edward said. "Her husband, Count Lorenzo Santini, had given it to her when he was courting her. He had it made in France and, and it bore his own and his mother's initials."

"LSS," said everyone.

"Lucretia Sassone Santini, and Lorenzo Sebastiano Santini," Edward elaborated. "Lorenzo had the word 'evermore' engraved before he gave it to Philippa. She adored the locket and never took it from her neck. Every year, she and her sister Lucetta had their photos taken, and Philippa put the new year's portrait in the locket."

"How do you know all that?" asked Chauncey, skeptically.

"It's in the report, sonny. See for yourself," said Edward, passing the papers to him.

"One year, Lucetta offered to take the locket to the A. M. Giroux photography studio to have the new portraits put in, and it was never seen after that," Chauncey read.

Edward, who had memorized the particulars of the story, continued, "Philippa assumed that someone at the photography studio had at best misplaced or at worst stolen the locket, and she launched an insurance claim. Not to be reimbursed for the price of the locket, but to recover the object."

"Lucetta had stolen it?" asked Helen with a gasp.

"No. Aubrey had," Edward continued. "Lucetta swears she brought it home, and there the trail goes cold…"

"…until," Chauncey exclaimed, reading the report, "the investigators came from New York and found several pieces of stolen jewelry in the Bowles home!"

"Philippa declined to press charges," Edward said, "and that was the end of the investigation into the locket."

"But was the locket recovered?" Helen asked.

"Philippa never saw it again," Edward answered.

"How did it come to be in Germaine's back yard, I wonder," Chauncey mused. "Aubrey had terrible gambling debts and he sold all the jewels he stole as soon as he could unload them. I doubt he would have sentimentally buried such a pricey bauble when he could have melted it down and paid off some debts."

"Look at the date of the insurance investigation findings," Edward instructed.

Chauncey did as he was told, and read the year out loud. "There's something familiar about that date," he said, "but I can't put my finger on it."

"It's the year that Aubrey and family moved to Boston," Germaine said.

"You know," Chauncey said, putting the insurance documents down, "things changed when A.B.One moved out of Springdale. There were no more gambling debts, and there were no more reports of the Swarthy Swiper."

"Perhaps he was so scared of the insurance investigation that he just stopped," Helen suggested.

"Perhaps," Chauncey chimed in, "but I think we need to take a closer look at the documents I brought home from the Bowles basement. It's too late now, but let's get an early start tomorrow."

The friends young and old all agreed to gather at 27 Trilby Street the following morning to try to put some of the pieces of the puzzle together.

"Mr. Bartlett," Helen said gently, "you said you knew even without the insurance documents that the jewels Viola

Bowles brought into your father's shop were Lucetta's. How do you know that?"

"Ah, my young librarian friend, how good of you not to let that remain unsaid! And, I think, you will like the answer because it involves scrupulous record-keeping," Edward said with a jolly smile as he took a thick stack of delicate papers from his breast pocket.

"This," he said, "is my father's account of his dealings with Viola Bowles. Filed in his records under Bowles, Viola." And with that introduction, Edward went on to tell a gripping story of how Viola came by her aunt's jewels.

"The Bowles moved to Boston after Philippa's locket was lost. Viola was quite young when they moved and had no memory of her aunt or of her family's life in Springdale. Viola's mother, Lucetta, died from influenza when Viola and her brother Aubrey Junior were in their teens. After their mother's death, Colonel Aubrey became even more distant, spending days away from home. He was prone to wild mood swings, and during a happy phase, he beckoned Viola into his study and presented her with what he said was her mother's legacy," Edward paused dramatically.

"The jewels!" exclaimed Chauncey, unable to restrain himself.

"Not just the jewels, sonny, the chest, too," said Edward, correcting the young interrupter.

"Do go on, Edward. We promise we won't interrupt you," Germaine said, giving Chauncey a poke in the ribs.

"Well, according to what Viola told my father, Colonel Aubrey said the jewels had been Lucetta's and that she always wanted to give them to Viola and pass them down through the female line of the family."

"The cad!" Chauncey hissed.

"Indeed. He also told her the jewels were not to be worn outside of their home," Edward went on.

"Why ever not?" asked Helen, as Germaine silently wished her friends would stop interrupting.

"He told her they were too valuable and they might make her the target of a thief," he said.

"Takes one to know one," muttered Chauncey.

"May I continue?" Edward asked. Chauncey nodded mutely.

"Well, Viola loved to look at the jewels and wear them around her room. One day she was putting the locket on," and here Edward paused to see if Chauncey planned to interrupt him. When there was no interruption, he continued with a smile, "and she found the second compartment. There was a note in it from Lorenzo to Philippa in which he pledged his love for ever more. Viola was devastated. Her father had told her the locket had been her mother's, and now it was clear it had been her aunt's.

"All her life, Viola's father had spoken ill of Lorenzo Santini. He had called him a thief, a liar, and a Papist. He pitied Philippa and said she'd been a fool to remain with her husband. He blamed Lorenzo Santini for Philippa's early death, and sometimes would even blame him for his own wife's untimely demise. Viola despised this sort of talk, and never brought her uncle's name up. She dared not ask her father about what she had found in the locket. Instead, she went to her brother, Aubrey Junior, and explained everything to him."

"Gosh," Germaine said, despite herself. "This isn't what I thought had happened."

"Over the course of several weeks, the siblings looked through boxes of things that their father had simply moved into the attic after their mother's death. There were letters and journals, newspaper clippings, photographs, and calling cards. Each day, when their father went out and about, the brother and sister would mount the stairs and piece together more information about the lives of their parents and their family. They learned that their father had forced their mother to break off relations with her sister when they moved to Boston, and that both sisters corresponded in secret, despite Colonel Aubrey's command that they have no contact. They read in these letters that Lorenzo Santini showered Philippa with gifts of jewelry, while Lucetta never received even a birthday card from her husband," said Edward, sometimes looking to his father's notes for confirmation of the tale.

"Through their careful and surreptitious investigations in the attic, the siblings concluded that the jewelry had been Philippa's. They couldn't understand why their father had tried to pass it off as Lucetta's, but they assumed that he might have felt embarrassed at not having given her such gifts when she was alive, and was attempting to repair that by telling his daughter that the jewels had been her mother's."

"So they didn't know their father was the Swiper?" Helen asked.

"All in good time, child, all in good time," Edward said, relishing his role as storyteller.

"Viola was in a quandary. She didn't want to upset her father, and at the same time, she didn't want to have possession of something that wasn't rightfully hers. She and Aubrey Junior agonized over the right course of action. In the end, fate decided for them. Colonel Aubrey Bowles died after being struck by lightning while crossing the street to his club one evening. After the estate was settled, Viola wanted to ascertain, once and for all, who was the rightful heir to the jewels."

"And that's when she came into Bartlett's Family Jewels," Germaine said, concluding the story.

"And that's when she came into Bartlett's Family Jewels," Edward repeated. "She was in mourning, which is why she was wearing black. It was about a year after her father died, and she and Aubrey Junior didn't want the jewels if they had not truly belonged to their mother."

"Were they Philippa's jewels?" asked Helen.

"Oh yes," Edward answered. "My father was able to find insurance records for almost all of the items, and they had been insured by Philippa Santini, née Sheppard."

"And when he told Viola, what did she do?" Chauncey asked.

"She asked my father to act as an intermediary. Rose was very young at the time, and as both of her parents were deceased, and the Santini and Bowles families were estranged, she had been sent to a boarding school. Viola asked my father to arrange for the chest of jewels to be restored to Miss Rose anonymously on her twenty-first birthday, which he did."

"And Miss Rose never knew that the jewels had been stolen?" Helen asked incredulously.

"No. While I'm no fan of the current Aubrey Bowles, I have to say that his father and Viola were truly kind people. They shielded Rose from the false rumors about her father.

They also kept quiet about their own father's less than sparkling actions in taking the jewels. I don't believe they ever knew he was the Swarthy Swiper," said Edward. "My father was instructed to tell her that the jewels had been kept safe for her until she reached her majority."

"And to think that you had seen this same locket so many years before and forgot all about it," Germaine said.

"Not all of us have that filing cabinet of a memory you have, Germaine," Edward Bartlett chuckled. "But what I do have are real filing cabinets full of my father's old records. I spent days reading through them until I came to the invoice that brought all those old memories back to me, clear as day, and brought me a lot of information that I would never have known."

"Well," said Germaine. "The pieces are all falling into place now. Miss Rose was definitely the rightful heir to the locket and the chest of jewels. I'm sure that the key in the locket opens the chest of jewels. Now, we just have to figure out if the chest and the jewels it once held still exist."

"I'd like to know how the locket made its way into the garden," Helen said.

"Germaine," said Chauncey, "I know that look of yours. You're on to something."

"I do have a few ideas," she said with a sweet smile, "but I shan't say more until I'm quite sure."

"I guess whatever you're thinking will be a mystery for the rest of us to solve. Just like how you got the locket back," said Helen. Germaine and Chauncey shared a smile.

Chapter Nineteen: Tea and Tablet

"I do hope you won't be too hard on her," Germaine Moreau said as she sat in her former professor's cluttered office. "I'm sure she was just trying to impress you with her speed as a researcher."

"Well she has done just the opposite," said Dr. Dupre crossly.

"Won't you let me speak with her for a moment?" Germaine asked. Dr. Dupre agreed, and Germaine went out in the hall and sat with Claudia Saunders.

"Claudia," Germaine said kindly, "much of the information you found about the Stevens family was correct, but it seems you jumped to an erroneous conclusion about the photos that we asked you to research."

Claudia said nothing and avoided Germaine's gaze.

"The people in the photographs were Philippa and Lucetta Sheppard, two sisters, not Harriet and Margaret Stevens. Would you tell me why you believed the photos were of the Stevenses?"

"Because they lived there!" Claudia cried. "I was sure it would be them. I wanted to get you an answer quickly and I was sure they were the women in the photos. Dr. Dupre is always talking about what a great researcher you are and I wanted to be as good as you," she said, her chin beginning to pucker.

"Claudia, I'm honored that you wanted to emulate me as a researcher," Germaine said, clasping the younger woman's hand. "But good research isn't the same as fast research. It can take weeks of sitting in the library, poring over documents before a researcher can even begin to find answers. Being slow is nothing to be ashamed of. To the contrary, slow and steady is the way to go when it comes to fact-finding." Germaine smiled at Claudia, whose tears were slowing.

"Is Dr. Dupre very angry at me?" Claudia asked timidly.

"Nothing a heartfelt apology won't fix," Germaine replied as she stood up. "I think you've learned a valuable lesson, and I'm glad it was nothing more serious than a few old photos." And with that, Germaine popped her head into Dr. Dupre's office, saw that he had cooled off, and sent Claudia in to apologize.

"Now I have my own research to do," she said, heading back to Springdale.

While Germaine was meeting with their old professor, Chauncey Fetterson was sketching out ideas for how he would have liked to have designed the new Bowles grave monument. Chauncey knew that Aubrey's father, Aubrey Bowles Junior, had been a kind and good man. He had been a big supporter of the local historical societies, both in Boston and Springdale. He was a bit of an amateur historian himself, and had a reputation as an expert in pre-Colombian figurative sculpture. But Chauncey found he had to banish all thoughts of Aubrey Junior from his mind as he sketched what would rightly be described as a monstrosity of a grave marker.

Chauncey kept the Colonel and the current bearer of the names Aubrey Bowles in his mind. He sketched a figure of a masked bandit sneaking off with a strand of pearls, and a fat industrialist stepping on factory workers. Chauncey laughed at his drawing with a snort, which caused Helen to look up with a start.

"What are you doing over there, Chauncey?" she asked, putting down the sisters' correspondence, which she had been re-reading to see if she could glean any clues about the whereabouts of the missing jewels.

"Voici!" exclaimed Chauncey with a grin, showing off his handiwork. Helen laughed, too. "Oh Chauncey, can you imagine?" she chuckled.

"What are you really thinking of designing?" she asked, making her way across his dining room to his dining room table headquarters, where he was sitting surrounded by piles of papers and photos.

"Something like this," he said, turning the page to a previously completed sketch in his large artist's notebook. It was granite and blended Rococo and Federal elements in a historically improbable fashion.

"Good grief, Chauncey," Helen said, putting her hand on her hip and frowning. "How can you have fluted columns and a triangle pediment with all those fat cherubs?"

"Because the customer requested it. I tried to convince him to stick to one style, but he wanted these elements specifically. I've simply tried to make it look as balanced as possible, in case anyone ever discovers that I designed it," replied Chauncey.

"What will they do with the old urn monument?" asked Edward Bartlett, who was looking over the insurance documents he had brought to Springdale from New York.

"Funny you should ask. I wondered if they'd like to incorporate it into the new monument for sentimental reasons, but A.B. Three told me to just get rid of it. I was thinking of bringing it here – it would look great in my back garden with some English ivy climbing up it," he answered. "Plus, it doesn't seem right to destroy a grave marker, even if it is being replaced with another."

"Well, since you are taking a break from your work, I dare say this is as good a time as any for you to try some tablet," said Arthur McTavish Fetterson, Chauncey's father, who let himself in the front door and placed the just cooled confection on the dining room table.

"Oh, Mr. Fetterson," Helen exclaimed, "I haven't had tablet since last summer. It looks divine!"

"And divine it is, lassie! I hope you like it; I make some up every year at about this time and leave some out in the garden for the fairie folk who are apt to appear in midsummer. So make sure you don't eat it all, or else the fairies will be after ye!" said Chauncey's father with a wink.

"I don't think we could eat all of this even if we tried," Helen said, eyeing the overflowing tray of tablet. "The only ingredients are sugar, butter, and cream, if I remember correctly. I think we would expire before we ate all the tablet you brought!"

"I'll make a pot of tea," said Chauncey. "Father, will you join us or do you have to rush back to the shop?"

"Aye, lad, I should like to sit and have a wee cuppa with my boy. Ta! And make sure you make enough for five," Mr. Fetterson said.

"Is that for the fairies, too?" asked Helen.

"No, it's for Germaine Moreau, who I saw driving this way with a big box in her car, and who, I am sure, is joining you in some sort of high-jinks as usual," said the celebrated Scottish baker, winking at Edward Bartlett.

As Mr. Fetterson finished speaking, the old-fashioned crank doorbell rang, and Chauncey rose to greet their friend, who was indeed carrying a large box.

"These are what I wanted to bring over the night I was locked in the secret room," she said, putting the box down and sitting with the little group for tea and tablet. "They're Miss Rose's diaries."

"Now that was a fine woman, Miss Rose," said the suddenly sentimental Mr. Fetterson. "Some called her eccentric, but I'll tell you young folks this, an unkind word never passed her lips. She stayed all alone in that big house of hers, but instead of shutting herself up like a hermit, she was always volunteering at the children's hospital. And she gave away all her money to one good cause or another."

Miss Rose Santini eventually had to leave her beloved house and move to a rest home when she became too frail to stay by herself. It was Germaine's parents who bought the Sheppard home from her, and with the sale, the house left the Sheppard family for the first time. Miss Rose interviewed all the prospective buyers of her home while lying in her little twin bed in the rest home, surrounded by antique lace pillows and doilies. While most who wanted to purchase the home were put off by the restrictions Miss Rose required of the garden, and while some found the woman herself a bit odd, the Moreaus were delighted with the house, the woman, and the task of gently and respectfully restoring it. Germaine's parents visited Miss Rose every week for the rest of her life, and they frequently brought her to the Sheppard house so that she could visit her old home and be assured that the Moreaus were working in accordance with her wishes.

"Now Germaine, your folks let that woman die in peace," Mr. Fetterson said, tears beginning to well up in his eyes as he thought of Germaine losing both her parents at such a young age.

"What did you want us to see in the journals?" asked Chauncey, to change the subject of discourse a bit.

"Well," Germaine said, picking up one of the books, "I think that there may be some mention of Viola's visit in these diaries. And that might give us a clue as to where the jewels are."

"I'll leave you to your sleuthing," said Chauncey's father as he put down his teacup and made his way out of the house.

"Miss Rose kept a daily diary, isn't that right?" asked Helen.

"It is," her friend responded. "First we need to read the entries around the time of Viola's visit, which according to you, Edward, should be about sixty years ago."

Chapter Twenty: A secret code

"Here it is," Helen exclaimed, holding up a well-preserved volume of Miss Rose's diaries.

May twenty-third. Received a strange surprise today. A note from Mr. Bartlett the jeweler indicating some mix-up in the shop. Mother had sent her jewels to Bartlett for storage and he came across them doing an inventory check. Rain today. Peonies are budding.

"Is the note from Bartlett's Family Jewels there?" asked Germaine. Helen shook the journal by its spine, and they all held their breath, but nothing fluttered out. "No," she answered.

"What a treat it would be to see my father's signature after all these years," Edward said.

"I'll keep reading," Helen replied.

Chauncey and Germaine were seated across from each other at one end of the dining room table. They were going through Lucetta and Philippa's correspondence to create a timeline of the letters the two sisters wrote to each other.

"And all she mentions is the letter from Edward's father?" Chauncey asked. "No jewels?"

"Not yet," Helen answered. "Stop interrupting me, please. I'll let you know when I find something."

Chauncey rolled his eyes and returned to the task he and Germaine were sharing. His eyes landed on the next letter in the stack. "That's odd," he muttered.

"What is?" Germaine's curiosity was piqued.

"This letter. It has notes in the margins in green ink. The ink is much brighter than the body of the letters, and they look like they're in code."

Germaine got up to get a better look at what Chauncey was describing. "It *is* odd," she agreed. "And I know the hand that made those encrypted notes. That is Miss Rose's handwriting. She had a distinctive version of the Spencerian ladies hand. I would know that writing anywhere." Germaine picked up one of the journals to compare the penmanship from the journal with that in the margins of the older letter. Edward and Chauncey agreed that Miss Rose's distinctive hand was responsible for the coded notations.

"Would you please keep it down? I can't read with you muttering in the background." Helen requested. Chauncey's dining room table was so large that they couldn't hear each other clearly from one end to the other without raising their voices.

"But Helen," Germaine said, knowing her friend's expertise in code cracking, "it's a secret code."

Helen rushed over, "Why didn't you say so before!" The smiling Germaine handed Helen the letter and Helen transcribed what was on the letter into a page of her special historian's notebook:

Dear Philippa, I'm so sorry we had a row. I'm even sorrier to admit you were right. Your suspicions about A. were correct. I have proof that even I cannot but believe. I don't know how I shall proceed. I am concerned about all. Oh dear Philippa… What shall I do?

Your loving sister,

Lucetta

On the margin was the following notation:

Q: W A S S. W D H H L.

"Chauncey," asked Helen, "would you please look through and see if you find any other letters from Lucetta with marks like these in the margins? You should too, Germaine."

As Germaine and Chauncey carefully examined their stacks of letters for other such messages, Helen scribbled out possible solutions to the code on a pad of paper. "Helen," Germaine said with excitement, "come have a look at this!" It was a tiny sheet of paper, folded several times, that had been tucked into one corner of a letter from Philippa.

The letter itself read:

Dearest sister, Please stop blaming yourself for all this. You are without fault, beloved, unless to love your husband is a fault, in which case we are equally guilty. It upsets me so to know you are distraught. I do wish I could see you, but I know it would only upset you more. I don't care a whit for those trinkets, only as reminders of L's love. But I need no such reminders, for he is in my heart evermore. You know how conflicted I was to display such gifts in public. This may be a better solution for all. If they can be useful for you and A to start afresh in Boston, then I am glad to be rid of them. I only ask that if you can, without problem, retrieve our last photos from the locket, I would be grateful for those reminders of happier times. I do hope we shall be able to visit soon. *You and the children are always welcome here, dearest sister.*

Yours,

Philippa

And in Miss Rose's distinctive hand, folded note read:

A S T J F M. A W A T.

"I can't make heads nor tales of it," Helen said. "I expected the initials to correspond in some way to the body of the letter. But they don't. It doesn't make any sense," she said with a sigh.

"What if we take a slightly different approach," asked Germaine. "Perhaps it's a different kind of code. When I was a child, I would often write notes to myself that I didn't want my parents to read. I would just write the first letter of each word in a sentence. Of course, sometimes I would find the notes and couldn't remember what the words were," she admitted with a chuckle.

"If we look at the first one, *Q: W A S S. W D H H L.* I'll bet the 'Q' stands for "question," Germaine said.

"And I bet 'A' stands for Aubrey One," said Chauncey.

"And SS could easily be the Swarthy Swiper," added Helen.

"Question: Was Aubrey Swarthy Swiper?" the three friends read in unison.

"So we weren't the first to wonder this," Chauncey said, amazed.

"No, Germaine responded. "Nor was Rose. Remember that Viola and Aubrey Two probably figured it out, too."

"Why didn't anyone go to the police?" Helen asked.

"People didn't go to the police in those days," Germaine answered.

"Unseemly," said Chauncey.

"Philippa was a gentle soul, much like her daughter Rose," Edward added. "She must have assumed that the police would get to the bottom of things and Aubrey would be discovered as the Swarthy Swiper. Philippa surely wanted to spare her sister any distress. That's what the letter is saying. Besides," he went on, "look what I found in the records Chauncey brought back from the Bowles' family archives." He pointed to an old will.

Chauncey was beside him and read it out loud, "I leave all my estate to my children, Viola and Aubrey Junior, to be held in trust by my husband until they reach their respective majorities. If I predecease my husband, he is to draw an allowance of not more than $1,000 per month from my estate, for the wellbeing of our children. He may not sell or otherwise dispose of any of my property during that time."

"I wonder if Lucetta knew he had stolen so many people's jewels?" Edward mused.

"It's hard to tell," Germaine replied. "But she certainly didn't trust Aubrey. And the letter proves that she knew he'd taken Philippa's jewels."

"Let's keep trying to crack this code," Helen urged. "I feel like the story is all coming together now."

"*W D H H L...* What does that one mean, Germaine?" Edward asked her friend with a smile.

"Frankly," Germaine frowned, "I don't know. I think the 'W' is another question word, maybe WD stands for 'who did' or 'what did' but I'm not sure." She put down the letter and looked over at Chauncey who was guessing words that might match with the letters on the folded paper.

"Aha!" he crowed, "Aubrey Stole The Jewels From Mother. *A S T J F M*. Hah!"

"Okay smarty pants," teased Germaine, "What's *A W A T*?"

"Aubrey Was Awfully Tall?" he guessed.

"No, but you're close. Aubrey Was A Thief," Helen said definitively.

"Now we're getting somewhere," Germaine said, encouragingly. "But what about that second one on the letter. *W D H H L*... I think the L must be for Lucetta or Lorenzo. Philippa was very concerned about Lucetta's well-being. I would hate to think it meant Why Did He Hurt Lucetta, but it could be."

"Or it could be Why Did He Hate Lorenzo," Chauncey added.

"Both worthy questions," Helen said. "I don't think we can decide on that one, but we've really cracked the code on the other notations."

"Hmmm…" Germaine said, sitting back down at the table. "What does it mean that Rose knew that her uncle stole her mother's jewels and cast aspersions on her father's good name?" she asked quietly.

"What I wonder is when she knew it and what she did with the jewels when she found out?" Edward asked. "She got the jewelry when she turned twenty-one, and she was still estranged from the Bowles family, so she wouldn't have been able to ask Viola about them. Besides, she didn't know the Bowles side of the family had taken temporary possession of them."

"Well, she clearly didn't destroy the letters," Chauncey said, "so I bet she didn't destroy the jewels either."

"I've just remembered something!" Germaine exclaimed with a start. "One of the first clues I found about this whole mystery was when I read over some of Miss Rose's old diaries. There was an entry about the family and jewels that Miss Rose said was too awful to put in writing. Hold on," she told her friends, as she quickly scanned the books to find the entry.

"Here it is! *Today I learned a somber story about the family and the jewels. I don't even dare to write it in my diary. But I will forget it not.*"

"Let's see if there is more information in her journals," Helen suggested. "Sometime between when she got the jewels at twenty one and when she wrote that entry at forty five, she clearly learned something. I'll divvy up the diaries and we can all scan for any mention of her discovery."

Each friend took several volumes and did their best to quickly pass their eyes over Miss Rose's neat and old-fashioned writing. The early entries were in faded fountain pen, and as time went by, that ink yielded to ballpoint pen. They searched for mentions of the locket, the case of jewels, Viola, the letters, or anything else that might help them figure out where Rose put the chest of jewels that had been her mother's.

"Germaine," Helen exclaimed, "I think I've found something."

Chapter Twenty One: A tidy sum

Germaine and Chauncey rushed over to Helen's side and listened as she read an entry that was written a few years before Miss Rose died.

October 17. I took care of the cursed jewels today. Those little bits of metal and stone had driven such a wedge in our family, and I felt constrained living under the same roof with them for so many years. Even though I had kept them in the hidden room, I still knew they were there, hanging over me as a reminder of family sorrows. I returned them to the Bowles family, where they were always more wanted than they were by Santinis. I'm keeping up a family tradition by putting them in Bowles hands... I hope those cursed jewels will never trouble anyone again. I kept the locket separate. It was mother's favorite. I have many photos of her wearing it, and she wears it in the portrait Mr. Benjamin painted. I buried the locket in the garden here; under forget-me-nots, mother's favorite. I wanted to take care of everything before the ground froze, but I couldn't resist a little whimsy. I finally feel free. I'm ready to die in peace.

Helen put down the slim volume and the three friends were silent.

"From the date of the entry, this happened about thirty-five years ago. A.B. Three was too young to have known anything, but Viola and A.B. Two would still have been alive," Chauncey guessed. "She must have given them back to them. A.B. Three must have them by now, though. Perhaps that's what he using to finance his campaign for senate."

"Or his new mausoleum," Helen added.

"Yes," Germaine said in an odd voice, "about that mausoleum… We have taken up so much of your time with this hunt for jewels, you've probably not made much headway on the new Bowles family monument."

"Au contraire, ma chére," Chauncey rejoined, francophonically. "Voici!" He exclaimed again, flourishing a large cardboard tube. And he expertly unrolled the plans for the new Bowles monument.

It was massive. There were carved granite columns, cherubs and birds, vines and leaves, an iron gate with intricate scrollwork, and topping everything was a huge brass B. The girls burst out laughing.

"Oh Chauncey, you *can't* be serious," Germaine laughed.

"You wound me," said he, deadpan. "I am as serious as the $300,000 that Mr. Aubrey Bowles the third is paying for my design. A tidy sum," he went on as the girls' jaws remained dropped, "that will allow me to purchase father's childhood home in Scotland." Germaine knew that the Fetterson family home in Aberdeen had been up for sale, and that the family wanted very much to purchase it, but couldn't come up with the money. Now she understood why Chauncey had produced something so garish and out of keeping with all his design principles. Sometimes, compromises did need to be made.

"But what if A.B. Three rejects this plan?" Helen said, fearing Chauncey might be getting his hopes up too quickly.

"He has seen it. He has loved it. He has approved it. And he has given me a check." Chauncey said, somewhat smugly. "The granite is being assembled in New Hampshire as we speak. Disinterment begins promptly on September first."

"Good grief. What are they going to do with the existing draped urn?" asked Germaine.

"I may do with it what I will. As I told Helen earlier, I thought it would make quite a nice addition to my garden. Something to remember the Bowles family by."

"Poor Aubrey Junior," said Edward. "First his father, now his son. Such disappointments. Well, they say things like this skip a generation, so perhaps when an Aubrey Four enters the picture, he'll be different."

"When will you pick the urn up?" Helen asked Chauncey.

"Any time I like. I think A.B. Three would like me to take it sooner than later so he can concoct some sort of story about the marker being stolen and simply replacing it with a new one in case anyone asks."

"Some replacement!" Helen snorted. "You're awfully quiet, Germaine. What's on your mind?"

"Oh, nothing… I'm just thinking about poor Miss Rose living all that time with the jewels in her house. I wonder if that's why she kept to the downstairs so much in her later years. Perhaps she couldn't face being closer to those jewels."

"When do you think she figured out the whole story of the Swarthy Swiper?" Chauncey asked, rolling his Bowles Monument design back up.

"I don't know, Chauncey. But I'm beginning to think that Viola may have played a part in that disclosure."

"It's awfully late, and I have to be up to work at the library bright and early tomorrow morning," Helen said with a yawn. "Can we put these to the side and call it a night?" Everyone agreed that they'd done enough reading and questioning for one day, and Edward needed to get back to Chalmsford. Germaine offered to drive Helen home. On the way, Helen questioned Germaine about the mystery, and when she thought Miss Rose had returned the jewels to the Bowles family, but Germaine just put her finger to her lips, indicating she would not divulge her thoughts just yet.

"I can use father's truck to bring the dreadful draped urn to my garden this afternoon. Helen has to work, but would you like to come with for the grave robbing?" Chauncey asked his friend Germaine Moreau over the telephone.

"Oh Chauncey, don't call it that!" she answered. "But yes, I'd love to help. I'll bring my camera so we can show Helen what she missed."

Germaine drove up to the modest Bowles family plot later that afternoon. She had arrived before Chauncey, so she parked her car to the side and snapped some photos of the burial site. Colonel Aubrey Bowles was buried there, along with Lucetta Sheppard Bowles, Aubrey Junior, and his wife Cynthia Tuttle Bowles. Germaine noticed that the year of Cynthia Bowles death was the same year that Rose had written her diary entry about returning the jewels to the family.

"Perhaps Miss Rose gave the jewels to Aubrey Three after Viola died," Germaine thought to herself. At that moment, she heard the wheels of Mr. Fetterson's truck rumbling up the gravel path in the cemetery. Chauncey parked the vehicle, and hopped out wearing white workers overalls.

"Hello, grave robber!" he called out with a mischievous smile. He held a smaller pair of white overalls in his outstretched hand. "Your grave robbing outfit, mademoiselle."

"Oh Chauncey," Germaine said somewhat crossly, "please stop saying that or I shall leave. Aubrey Three asked you to take this away, and he notified the proper cemetery officials, so this is hardly grave robbing."

"Germaine, you're taking all the fun out of it."

She stepped into the overalls as Chauncey promised to come up with another name for their cemetery adventure.

"What do you think the urn is made of?" he asked, approaching the plot. "Granite or cement?"

"I don't know. Cement can be made to seem like granite in a skilled artisan's hands," she said, snapping a photo of Chauncey in his overalls. "And the Bowles family had fallen on hard times. Plus the children probably didn't want to call attention to the grave, once they knew that Aubrey One was the Swarthy Swiper," she said taking a photo of the grave site before they attempted their renovation. "We'll know when we lift it, though! Hold on and I'll give you a hand." She put down the camera and stood opposite her friend at the monument. Chauncey had brought a hand-truck up to the edge of the grave, and they planned to lift it up and wheel it to the truck.

"One, two, three!" he instructed as they each picked up one end.

On three, the two heaved with all their might and were surprised at how light the draped urn was.

"All that lemonade we've been drinking seems to have given us super-human strength," Chauncey said as they easily carried the monument to the hand-truck. When they placed it down, though, they both heard a distinct second thud.

"What was that?" asked Chauncey as Germaine, who had a very good idea of what it was, furiously turned the monument by its handles.

"You hold the bottom part still," she told her friend. She continued turning until the upper part of the urn came off.

Both friends peered into the hollowed out urn and stepped back in unison. "The jewels!"

Chapter Twenty Two: "We've found them!"

"Germaine! We've found them!" Chauncey was practically jumping for joy. He noticed that his friend seemed strangely calm. "If you tell me that you knew they were here all along, I'm going to be seriously disappointed that you didn't tell me. Or Helen, for that matter."

"I had a suspicion, but I didn't *know* they were here," she answered. "So save your disappointment. You may need it if we open the box and it's empty." Germaine smiled sweetly.

"Well, promise me that you will tell me whence your suspicion arose."

"I promise, but let's talk about that later. With Helen." Germaine was eager to open the chest and find out if the jewels were indeed inside. She carefully removed a square object wrapped in coarse burlap. Beneath that was a finer fabric, that was still quite a vibrant white.

"Muslin or linen, what's your guess?" Germaine asked, slowly removing the fabric.

"Germaine! Open it!" Chauncey demanded with utter exasperation.

"This is the same way the letters were wrapped that were hidden in the fireplace. Fine linen surrounded by burlap. I believe this is Miss Rose's handiwork," she smiled and laid the coarse and the fine fabric to one side and extracted the chest from the hollow urn. "Ta da," she said, quietly as she held the chest up so that she and Chauncey could examine it.

"Just like Edward's description," Chauncey said, remembering Edward Bartlett's description of Viola's visit to his shop so many years ago. "Gilded wood with pearl and lapis lazuli inlaid. It's beautiful."

"It is," Germaine agreed. "The bands are solid gold," she went on, inspecting the strips of precious metal that held the wood in place. "It does indeed look like Russian work. The metalsmithing is so fine." Germaine turned the chest over to examine it from every angle, with Chauncey looking over her shoulder.

Chauncey and Germaine had seen many treasures in museums and private hands in their years as historians, but neither had ever seen anything quite as exquisite as this jewelry chest. The light of the sun made the piece glow.

"Did you bring the key?" Chauncey asked, imagining the precious jewels inside.

Germaine shook her head. "I wasn't certain that the chest would be in the urn. It was just a hunch, so I didn't bring the key." Germaine looked around the cemetery. "Plus, I wasn't sure we would be alone. I didn't want to start pulling rubies and emeralds and opals out in such a public place."

Chauncey looked around, too, but there was no one else at the cemetery. The caretakers only worked on weekdays and most visitors came on Sundays. He was almost tempted to pry the chest open or try to pick the lock right there. But he knew Germaine wouldn't stand for it, and he didn't want to run the risk of damaging the chest.

"Well, let's get the urn in the truck and head back to town. I can't wait to see Helen's face when we tell her we've found the jewels!" and with that, Chauncey managed to lift the hollowed-out urn single-handedly into the back of his father's truck. He and Germaine secured the concrete monument with straps to be sure it wouldn't topple over as they drove. They closed and latched the sturdy metal doors on the back of the truck and hopped in the front. Germaine wrapped the chest back up in the muslin and burlap and held it carefully on her lap. As Chauncey fastened his seatbelt, Germaine adjusted the side mirror slightly.

Chauncey drove slowly over the gravel path that lead out of the cemetery. He was concentrating on avoiding the ruts and gulches in the unpaved road, and neither he nor Germaine spoke. Once he reached the road, though, he started chattering on about the jewels, and Edward Bartlett's descriptions of the jewels. Germaine had her eyes fixed on the mirror and was only giving brief yeses and nos as answers.

"I'm surprised that you aren't more excited about finding the jewels," Chauncey said.

"I'm thrilled that we have found this chest," Germaine replied, her eyes still on the mirror. "I just have a feeling that we aren't the only ones who know about it."

"Whatever do you mean?" Chauncey asked with utter surprise.

"I was in town the other day, and I saw Pugsy Littleton skulking about."

"Oh! So your little chat with him about listening in at windows and locking people in attics didn't have the intended effect?" Chauncey said, recalling the evening when he and Germaine retrieved the locket from him in his squalid home.

"I'm afraid not," she said, truly saddened that her efforts at turning the young man towards a better way in life seemed to have failed.

"I thought he looked very suspicious, so I followed him. I kept my distance so he wouldn't see me, and I was wearing a sunhat, which I pulled down over my face as much as I could. I even took a page from your book and tried to disguise my gait."

Chauncey cringed at the memory of how he had tried to deceive Germaine in the cemetery. "Go on," he said, as his flush faded.

"Well, he sort of skulked about for a while, then he went into the Princess Parlor on Main Street."

"Did you go in? That ice cream shop is so small there's no way he wouldn't notice you."

"I couldn't go in for just that reason. But Poli's Jewelry is next door, so I pretended to look at the jewelry in the window. The clerk was holding up a mirror for a customer inside and I saw the reflection of a familiar person enter the ice cream parlor."

"Who?"

"Guess."

"The ghost of Colonel Aubrey Bowles. I don't know, tell me!" Chauncey hated it when Germaine didn't get right to the point.

"You're almost right," she said. "It was Aubrey Bowles the third."

"A.B. Three?" Chauncey was flabbergasted. "I'm flabbergasted," he said.

"None other. Of course, he doesn't know me from a hole in the wall, but I've seen his face on enough campaign advertisements to recognize him anywhere."

"But he can't have been going to meet Pugsy?"

"Oh can't he have? I went into the jewelry shop and told one of the girls behind the counter that I would give her

$20.00 if she would go next door and pick up a cone of chocolate chip for me. I told her I had been on a few dates with Aubrey Bowles and if he saw me, I'd never get away from talking to him and I had an appointment to keep at the hairdresser's which is why I was wearing that hat."

"Wow, and she bought that?"

"Who knows, but she went and got me the ice cream," Germaine said, with a twinkle in her eye. "I thought that if I mentioned Aubrey Bowles she would pay special attention to him when she got me my cone."

"And were you right as always?" Chauncey asked, admiring Germaine's ability to understand people and think on her feet.

"Well, I was right that time," she replied modestly. "The girl came back with the ice cream and as I gave her the $20.00, she started telling me all about Aubrey Bowles and what he was wearing. But she also told me he was talking to a little boy and she said she heard Aubrey say something about jewelry, so she thought he would be coming in the store to buy something for me.

"She suggested I leave through the back door, and I thought I would seem suspicious if I declined, so I did go out the back and circled around the front just in time to see Aubrey and Pugsy leaving the ice cream parlor at the same time. Pugsy's pocket was bulging as he left, and he was swaggering down the street."

"Had A.B. Three paid him off?" Chauncey asked, amazed at this latest twist in the story.

"I think Pugsy approached Aubrey. Remember how some of the newspaper articles were gone from the house? I believe that Pugsy is either blackmailing the Bowles family about the Colonel being the Swarthy Swiper or that he has told Aubrey the third about the Sheppard treasure. Aubrey's face is everywhere while he's campaigning, so I bet Pugsy recognized the name and resemblance and gave Aubrey a call."

"Well it's certainly unsavory either way. So whom did you follow?"

"Pugsy knew me, so I decided to follow Aubrey. I could get closer to him with no chance of being recognized."

"Too bad you couldn't lure some passerby into tailing the kid. Did that sound like a hard-boiled detective talking?"

Germaine rolled her eyes and said, "Guess where Aubrey went."

"Germaine! Don't do that! Just tell me and stop making me guess!" Chauncey said in complete exasperation.

"Not even one little guess?" Chauncey's response was silence. "Okay, he went to the *Gazette*'s office."

"The newspaper?"

"None other. And he went straight downstairs to the archives."

"Was Doc working?"

"He was, so I knew I could find out what Aubrey was up to from him. I made sure he didn't see me, and I sat outside and finished my ice cream cone. It was very good."

"Was he in there long?" Chauncey asked, knowing that the man who worked in the newspaper archives, whom everyone called "Doc" could be garrulous or taciturn, helpful or stonily silent, depending completely on his whim. However, he had a soft spot for Germaine and gave her his undivided attention whenever she needed information from the newspaper archives. If Chauncey needed information from the *Gazette* archives, he always attempted to lure Germaine to accompany him with the promise of a visit to the nearby natural history museum, a particular favorite of hers.

"Not long at all. I figured he'd waved his name around and Doc gave him the old silent treatment, because he looked really cross when he left. I would normally ask you to guess where he went next, but my sleuthing skills tell me you're not interested in playing that guessing game."

"Thank you for your consideration," Chauncey said with a smile.

"Well, his next and final stop in Springdale was City Hall. The Clerk's office. I had some building permit paperwork I had agreed to drop off for Mrs. Clovington, so I waited in line behind him. He didn't look around or make small talk with anyone in the line. He had a great singularity of focus. And a great loud voice, so I didn't have to do a thing but stand there and listen."

"I bet he wasn't after a dog license."

"No, he wasn't. He asked the clerk for all records pertaining to the ownership of the property at 32 Beaumont, and copies of the Sheppard family wills."

"Why on earth would he think the City Clerk would have people's wills?" Chauncey asked, disappointed in the candidate's slim knowledge of the responsibilities of municipal departments.

"Well he blustered about with all sorts of 'do you know who I am?' nonsense, but the Clerk sent him to the Probate records department in the Courthouse. No one else in line would make eye contact with him. I was trying to be unobtrusive, but everyone else just seemed embarrassed for him," Germaine went on.

"So next stop, the courthouse?" Chauncey asked, visualizing the route Germaine took following Aubrey Bowles the third for several blocks through Springdale's bustling downtown.

"My thoughts exactly. I was even prepared to sacrifice my sunhat in the pursuit of truth and justice. I thought that even someone as distracted as he was couldn't have failed to notice me and my big hat in the same place twice. I was looking for someplace en route to the courthouse to hide my hat when he went in the other direction. He stomped off to his car and drove away."

"No courthouse?"

"No courthouse. I expect he had some other appointment to get to, and decided it wasn't worth his valuable time to look at dusty old wills. He can surely get one of his underlings to find the wills for him."

"And he probably wouldn't even know how to go about looking for them anyway," Chauncey added. The filing system was quite arcane and unless a person had experience in probate research, it could take hours to locate one document.

"No," Germaine agreed. "But I would."

Chauncey turned in the driver's seat to look at his friend and he saw a worried crease in her forehead as she continued staring into the side mirror. "What did you find?"

Chapter Twenty Three: Inside the chest

"I made copies of all the documents and have them at home. Let's look at them tonight when Helen has finished working. Three heads are better than one, as the old saying goes," Germaine said, trying to sound cheerful. As she said this, she continued keeping her eyes on the mirror.

"Who do you expect to be following us, exactly? Pugsy Littleton on his bicycle?" Chauncey asked.

"Maybe," Germaine smiled.

At last, the pair pulled into the alleyway behind Chauncey Fetterson's townhouse. "I don't think we were followed Germaine, so you should be able to help me unload the urn without any distracting thoughts."

Chauncey had hopped down from the truck and opened the ornate cast iron gate to his back garden. It was a small but elegant space, filled with boxwoods, lilacs, and hydrangeas. Chauncey's garden had a small bubbling fountain in one corner, and he planned to install the draped urn in the corner opposite the fountain. He had moved all the potted plants from that area and cleared a space for the monument on the flagstones that lined the ground. He had planted a weeping willow in the same corner a few years earlier.

"My goodness Chauncey, it's as if the garden was just waiting for this addition. What a lovely nook this will make in your little garden."

"I agree," Chauncey said. "That's why I leapt at the chance to take the urn when A.B. Three said he didn't want it. Little did I know what we would find inside the urn!"

"Speaking of which, let's get this thing situated so we can discuss the jewels and their dispensation," Germaine said, pulling on her work gloves and heading to the back of the truck.

Chauncey brought the hand-truck over and the two lifted the urn out of the truck and onto the dolly. It was easy for the strong and competent pair to wheel the dolly over to the corner and install the urn in the corner spot. They carefully replaced the top section that had lifted off to reveal the jewelry chest, and stood back to admire the object in its new location.

After a few moments of silent admiration, Chauncey rotated the urn ever so slightly to the right. "There!" he said.

"Perfect," the two friends said in unison.

*   *   *

"Oh, it's beautiful," Helen whispered as Germaine unwrapped the final layer of fabric from around the chest. "Pearls certainly do become more subtly beautiful as they age," she went on, gently caressing one of the cabochons on the box. "And that lapis is like looking into the night sky. When do you think it was made?"

"Edward dated the key to the mid-1600's and he thought it was Russian, even though the locket was made in France. I'm not a jewelry expert, but I think the scrollwork in the gold hinges is distinctly Russian. We'll know for sure when we bring it to Edward. He can look through catalogs and give a more definite date," Germaine said. After the three friends had examined the exterior of the ornate chest, Germaine took out the golden locket and laid it on the library table, next to the chest. She had turned on the lights in the room, and the electric glow that was reflected in the gold and jewels gave the chest a warm glow.

She opened the hidden compartment of the locket and gently removed the key. She kept the locket open to the photographs of Philippa and Lucetta, and addressed them saying, "You might like to witness this." Very carefully, she put the key in the lock. All three held their breath as the key turned. Germaine slowly opened the lid, and Chauncey and Helen strained to see the contents. The inner part of the lid was just as ornate as the outside. The design of pearls, gold, and lapis lazuli continued. The gold on the inside shined even more brightly, as it had been less exposed to the elements. All three friends exhaled when they saw that there was another piece of the chest obscuring the jewels it was designed to hold.

A tray of solid, hammered gold was perfectly fitted into the top of the chest. This tray would have held rings and bracelets and even earrings when the chest was safely installed in a lady's dressing room, but it served as extra protection for the lady's precious jewels when she travelled with the chest. The tray was further proof that the chest was likely to be from the middle of the seventeenth century, when the aristocracy was often obliged to travel in a hurry due to wars, plagues, and uprisings.

This chest would have kept a tsarina's or a princess's treasures quite safe.

Germaine lifted the tray out of the chest and took a wavering step backwards. Chauncey rushed to her side as he thought she was going to faint. Her knees buckled, but then she steadied herself. Helen and Chauncey looked at each other in concern before they peered past Germaine and into the chest. They gasped. There were no jewels in the chest. The only thing inside that precious box was a single sheet of paper.

Chapter Twenty Four: At last

It took the three friends a few moments to regain their composure. Helen and Chauncey both spoke at the same time. "Where could they be?" and "What does the paper say?" they asked.

Germaine held the paper in her hand in utter disbelief. "I was so sure that Miss Rose had put the jewels in the Bowles monument. So sure," her voice trailed off as she looked into the empty chest. She raised her hand to her face, and in so doing, realized the paper was in her hand. She read its words to herself, then straightened up and said to her friends sharply, "Listen to this!"

I, Rose Santini, being of sound mind and body, do hereby declare this to be my last will and testament. This document supersedes all previous wills and testaments, specifically the one filed in Springdale Probate Court, which left all my estate to the surviving members of the Bowles family. I will all the proceeds from the sale of my family home at 32 Beaumont Street to the Springdale Historical Society. I hereby will my entire estate at death to the Springdale Historical Society to use as follows:

Jewelry — the large collection of antique jewelry that is part of my estate should be displayed at the Springdale Historical Society with complete historical information about each piece.

Journals — the daily journals I kept throughout my life should be kept together, and may be displayed or used for research purposes. If excerpts from the journals are published, it is my express wish that all names be omitted and all people be referred to simply by initials.

Stocks and Bonds — the Society may use any liquid funds in the estate at the time of my death in any way they choose that is in keeping with the Society's mission.

Haberdashery — the entire collection of hats and trimmings that I have are to be displayed in the Society's museum as part of the permanent collection.

Witnessed by Jebidaih Sharpe, attorney at law.

"And it's signed Rose Santini, but then there is a little star next to her name, and something written on the back in green ink!"

"Oh, Germaine, what does it say?" Helen could barely contain herself.

Germaine read the note aloud. Miss Rose's spidery but strong handwriting was easy to make out:

<u>You</u> <u>are</u> <u>in</u> the right place, my friend. The jewels are <u>safe</u>. You <u>may</u> <u>pull</u> them down from garden. My <u>will</u> is resolute. I want them to go where they will do no harm. R.S.S.

"The words that are underlined are: *you, are, in, safe, may, pull,* and *will.* Helen, you're the code cracker. What do you think it means?"

"Germaine is there a maple tree in your back yard?" Helen asked, by way of response.

"Yes," Germaine answered. "You can see it from here." She pointed to the lovely old maple shading a cozy sitting area in the back of her house.

"You are in," Helen said. "U R N – urn, she was telling us to look in the urn. She must have hidden the letters at the same time when she hid the chest."

"But the note was in the urn!" Germaine said.

"Maybe she changed her mind about where she was going to leave the chest," Helen responded.

"Okay, but what about the jewels?" Chauncey asked.

"They're in the maple tree," both Helen and Germaine said.

"May pull, maple, okay, I get it, but how do you hide jewels in a tree?" Chauncey asked, scratching his head.

"There's some sort of a safe in or around the tree," answered Germaine. "That's why she underlined that word. Let's see what we can find." And with that, the three went outside and headed towards the majestic old maple tree, unsure of where or how the jewels could be.

"I'm stumped," said Chauncey with a grin. The girls rolled their eyes at his pun and inspected the old maple. The tree was clearly a real, healthy, living organism. They felt the bark to see if there had been some sort of door carved into it, but it was just a solid tree. They looked up into the branches to see if there were diamonds and emeralds entwined with the branches. Nothing.

"What a let-down," Chauncey said, dejectedly. "I was so excited when we heard the thud in the urn. Or should I say the 'you are in'," he said, smiling wanly.

"Are you really giving up just like that?" Germaine asked with genuine surprise. "The jewels are certainly somewhere around this tree. It is getting late and the light is fading, but I know the jewels are here somewhere. Miss Rose's message was clear."

"Well, I am giving up," Helen said. "At least for tonight." Chauncey seconded. "Besides, what if Pugsy already found it?"

"I don't think he has. I for one will be back here tomorrow. With a shovel and a ladder. And with Andrew McGrath to help me. You two are very welcome to join me, but if I find the treasure while you are still in bed, I'll wait until after 9:00 to call," Germaine said, her eyes twinkling.

And she was true to her word. The next morning, Germaine, as always, rose early. She prepared breakfast and looked through the many requests for help with historical decoration that she had received recently. She replied to some that she would not be able to help them, but included suggestions of other experts to contact. She required more information from some of the museums and homeowners before she could give a definite answer, so she requested that information. And some inquiries were precisely the sort of work that she loved to do, and to those she responded with a proposed schedule of work. All of her correspondence was done on creamy linen stationery with a small GM in the upper right hand corner. Once she had sealed and stamped the final envelope and put the entire stack of letters in the outgoing mail slot, she checked the time and saw that Andrew McGrath would soon arrive.

Germaine walked briskly to her dressing room and changed into her outdoor work outfit of denim jeans and long sleeves. She checked in the mirror to see that there were no un-patched holes in her laboring clothes, and when she was satisfied that she was both presentable and sensibly attired, she made her way to the back yard.

"Good morning, Miss Germaine," Andrew said, taking pride in the fine work he had done in the garden so far.

"Good morning, Andrew. My, you have done a wonderful job back here. Miss Rose would be as proud as I am of you," she said with a kind smile.

Andrew puffed his chest out a bit, happy for the deserved recognition of the hard work he had done. When Germaine explained that she was looking for some sort of secret hiding place in the old maple tree, Andrew quickly joined in the search. He brought out a very tall ladder from the shed, and although he would have preferred to have climbed up the tree and hoped very much that Miss Germaine wouldn't hurt herself – or worse yet – fall from the tree, he did as she instructed and held the ladder very steady as she disappeared into the tree.

Germaine was quite sure that Miss Rose's message *you may pull them down* meant that the jewels were hidden somewhere inside the tree, not buried beneath it. Just as the locket was under the forget-me-nots, she was certain that the jewels were *safe* in the tree. But where?

She carefully felt every inch of the bark. The secret hiding places in the house were so ingenious that Germaine quite expected to find a hidden mechanism that would spring open a door in the tree. She poked and prodded all the branches. "Perhaps *may pull* had a second meaning and I'm meant to *pull* on one of the branches to work a secret hinge," she thought to herself. When she had put her hands on every inch of the tree that could be reached while still on the ladder, she rested for a moment in exasperation and wiped her forehead. She looked up to gauge whether she would be able to climb higher into the tree by using the limbs to balance on, and as she did, something glinted in the sun. She took her breath in sharply and climbed up. Expertly moving from branch to branch, she scaled several levels of the tree until she found a hollow area where the reflection had come from.

She reached her hand in, and let out a cry of pleasure when her fingers touched cool metal. She opened her palm and revealed an exquisite diamond brooch. It was in the shape of a flower and each delicate petal was mounted on a spring, so they trembled ever so slightly in Germaine's hand. She carefully placed the brooch in one pocket of her overalls, and reached in again and again. Each dip into the hollow of the tree brought out exquisite and precious necklaces and earrings, bracelets and brooches, rings and combs. Some stones weren't even set in jewelry, they just lay there in the tree in perfect polished beauty. Germaine put handful after handful of the treasure into her pockets. When she came to the end of the jewels, she felt about for one last treasure, which she was quite sure she would find.

Dear friend, the note said, in Miss Rose's spidery hand, *you followed the clues in the letter and chest and you have found my family's treasure. There is no doubt in my mind that you know the awful secrets behind these jewels and the terrible pain they caused my family. Please dispose of them according to my wishes. Give them to the Historical Society, but do not tell them the tragic story of the jewels. I would like that chapter of history to be closed. Let the true identity of the thief remain a mystery. I don't want to cause any more pain.*

"Oh Miss Rose," Germaine said, her eyes welling up a bit, "You were so kind and gentle. How like you to be concerned for the Bowles family, even though the Colonel so wronged your poor father." But Germaine would never have disobeyed Miss Rose's wishes, so as she made her way back down the ladder, she knew she would keep the note secret, but give the will and the jewels and chest to the trustees of the Springdale Historical Society and see to it that Miss Rose's wishes were carried out to the letter. She was a bit preoccupied with wondering where the large haberdashery collection might be, and thought it wouldn't have survived very well if it, too, had been hidden in a tree. Her mind was so filled with thoughts of trees full of hats that she didn't notice that it was no longer the young and trustworthy Andrew McGrath who was holding the bottom of the ladder, but a quite different man wearing a uniform.

"Put your hands up in the air, please miss," the man said, and seemed somewhat embarrassed to be making such a command. He looked over to someone who Germaine took to be his supervisor, as he was dressed in a poorly-made and ill-fitting suit.

"Don't be ridiculous Regan," the man in the suit snapped. "You don't have to put your hands up, miss.

"Are you Germaine Moreau?" the man in the suit then asked. She naturally replied in the affirmative.

"We have an order here to seize any and all property on the premises that might rightfully belong to the Bowles family, Aubrey Bowles the third, or heirs of Bowles decedents," the man said, in an almost apologetic tone. He then fumbled to show Germaine a badge that identified him as the county sheriff.

"May I see that order, Sheriff?" Germaine said, climbing down the tree slowly to take the document. She noticed that there were two uniformed men in the yard, and that the one who hadn't been holding the ladder was standing next to and scowling at Andrew McGrath. Andrew looked very upset and Germaine wondered what sort of treatment the constables might have given him while she was in the tree.

Germaine read the document and saw that it had been issued the previous day. It referred to Miss Rose's old will which named the Bowles family as heirs to her estate. The document said that the Bowles family had reason to believe that Germaine Moreau was in possession of certain valuable pieces of jewelry that were part of the Sheppard-Santini estate, and that rightfully belonged to the Bowles. Germaine looked at the sheriff in disbelief. "Sheriff, how could anyone think that I would keep anything that was not rightfully mine?" she asked.

"Miss, I don't think anything about anything. We're just here to fulfill that court order." He looked down at his shoes. "This is a beautiful garden," he added. "You're doing a fine job, son," he said, nodding towards Andrew McGrath, who mumbled his thanks.

"Miss Moreau, my father was the Sheriff before me. There were a lot fewer people in Springdale in those days, and he knew all the important families pretty well. He always had very kind things to say about the Bowles and about Miss Rose. I know how much good Miss Rose especially did for the city, what with the museum and all." Germaine was impressed that the Sheriff knew about Miss Rose's philanthropic efforts, and she reminded herself not to judge a book by its cover. She remembered that she wasn't dressed very well herself, and the sheriff probably had a family to take care of, and no real need for tailored suits.

"I am sure this is just a misunderstanding and Mr. Bowles somehow got the wrong idea," he went on. "We'll just do a quick search and be on our way."

"Mr. Bowles did get the wrong idea," Germaine replied, "but not about me having the jewels. Come in the house with me, Sheriff. Can we leave the constables outside? This is a rather delicate matter."

He nodded, and followed her in. As he walked behind her towards the library, he noted his appreciation of several of the Hudson River School paintings that hung in the hallway, and said that Jerome Thompson was one of his favorite painters, and not only because he had been a soldier. Germaine was sure that the sheriff's surprising cultural refinement would make him a sympathetic listener.

She opened the jewel chest, which she had left unlocked, and removed Miss Rose's final, hand-written will. She handed him the will, and as he read it, she extracted the priceless antique jewels she had found in the tree and stored in her overalls. She then gently placed each unique jewel in the chest.

When the sheriff finished reading the will, he looked over at Germaine and his jaw dropped as he saw the treasures she was handling.

"You see, Sheriff, my involvement in this story began a few weeks ago when I decided to tidy up the garden," Germaine began. She told the sheriff almost the entire story, and he listened to her attentively, occasionally jotting things down in a small notebook. She omitted all references to the Swarthy

Swiper and the jewels having been stolen, but did tell him that the jewels changed hands from Sheppards to Santinis to Bowles, but that there was plenty of insurance documentation showing that Miss Rose was the rightful owner of the jewels. "And so I believe that the jewels, and the chest, and the hats, wherever they might be, all belong to the Springdale Historical Society. And I suppose if Aubrey Bowles the third, or any of the Bowles for that matter, were desperately poor, I would understand that they would want the jewels, but the Bowles are one of the wealthiest families in New England," she concluded. "Perhaps they want them for sentimental reasons?" Germaine said mischievously.

The sheriff smiled, "I don't think sentiment is entering into this on their end. Your case sounds very convincing, Miss Moreau, and I have no reason to believe this document is not authentic," he said, indicating the hand-written will. "But I have to carry out this order as it is written. Which means I have to seize the jewels."

Chapter Twenty Five: Last will and testament

"You found the jewels?" Chauncey asked, nearly barging into the room, and at the very least entering the room with more bluster than was strictly necessary. "Good heavens Germaine, what are you wearing?" he asked with deep concern.

"I was gardening. Sheriff Archer, Chauncey Fetterson," she said, introducing the two men. "In addition to being the County Sheriff, Mr. Archer is very knowledgeable about Jerome Thompson," she said, turning to Chauncey. "And Mr. Fetterson," she said, turning to the sheriff, "is an architect. One of his current projects is designing the new grave marker for the Bowles family," Germaine said, indicating that she had taken the Sheriff into her confidence. Chauncey blushed.

"Ah," the sheriff said with a nod. "So you are the one who is currently in possession of the hollowed out urn. We may have to examine that."

"You seem to know all about it," Chauncey said, arching his eyebrow.

"I have told the Sheriff how it was that I found the jewels and why it is that I believe they should be given to the Historical Society," said Germaine to her friend.

"Well where did you find them after all?" Chauncey asked.

"In the tree," the Sheriff answered before Germaine could.

"Just like the note said," she continued. "The dried maple leaf in the locket was another clue, but I didn't realize it until I got up in the tree."

"Well gentlemen," Germaine said, noting a bit of tension in the air, "I am sure we can settle this whole misunderstanding over Miss Rose's estate, and give the jewels to the museum, where they can be enjoyed by the public. Let's go downstairs and have a nice cup of tea, shall we? You two go downstairs, and I will change into something slightly more presentable. Mrs. White must have arrived by now. Chauncey, won't you ask her to serve tea and cake in the parlor? And please ask her to send some out to Andrew and the constables."

"Very well, miss. But I still have to take the jewels," said Sheriff Archer.

"We'll see. You and Mr. Fetterson can certainly take them downstairs and begin cataloging the contents. It seems most fortunate to have two sets of eyes to work on the task," she said sweetly.

Chauncey led the way and the sheriff carried the chest. Chauncey knew where Germaine kept lined paper, so he took out a few sheets and a pencil, and brought them into the parlor. He excused himself briefly to ask Mrs. White to serve the food Germaine had requested, and he told her they would explain everything later, but he didn't want to leave the sheriff alone with the jewels for too long. Mrs. White agreed.

Meanwhile, Germaine quickly changed into an attractive wool suit. She brushed her hair and examined her fingers for any signs of dirt or bark, and then sat down at the desk in the library to phone her attorney. She paged through the small tabbed address book until she arrived at the letter P. Germaine dialed Leonora Parker's number and the phone was picked up by Attorney Parker's secretary, Irene. Irene put Germaine straight through to the attorney, and Germaine briefly explained the situation. Leonora agreed to come right over to see if she could do anything to stall or stop the sheriff from taking the jewels.

"But if they have a court order, there may not be anything I can do," she said.

Germaine joined Chauncey and the sheriff in the parlor. The sheriff rose when she entered, and Chauncey quickly imitated the good manners of the other man, even though he, Helen, and Germaine were close enough friends that he didn't normally rise when either entered a room. Germaine smiled at both men and gracefully sat on a velvet wing chair. "How is the inventory coming along, gentlemen?" she asked, sipping a cup of tea.

"We are about halfway there," Chauncey replied. "It took us a while to agree on a system," he said, grinning at the sheriff, then at Germaine. "We are numbering each piece, then we both do our best to describe the item. The sheriff has sent for a photographer to come in and make a photo of each piece, too."

"Good idea," Germaine said, wanting to be certain that none of the jewelry went missing if Aubrey Bowles the third did somehow get his hands on it. She was pleased to see that the two men were working well together, and she was amused by some of the descriptions they were making of the jewels. "It's a good thing a photographer is coming," she thought to herself, "or no one would make heads nor tails of their descriptions. 'A dangly thing that is yellow and looks like a thermometer' is not exactly how I would describe a Tiffany tear drop pin." The doorbell rang, and Mrs. White showed Leonora Parker into the parlor.

The men rose, and Germaine made the introductions. "I thought it would be helpful for Attorney Parker to look over all the documents and see if we can save the sheriff's department the trouble of safeguarding the jewels if it's clear that the jewels should go to the museum, as Miss Rose's will clearly states" she said, in a straightforward manner.

"Miss Moreau, Attorney Parker is very welcome to review all of these documents, but I still have to remove the property according to this court order. I'm sorry for the inconvenience," he said.

As the men continued indexing the jewelry, Germaine and Leonora pored over the court order, the will that was in the jewelry chest, and notarized copies of the Sheppard, Santini, and Bowles wills, which she had gotten from the clerk at the office of probate records. Germaine asked Leonora to join her in the kitchen for a moment, so she could show her the old maple tree where the jewels were found and the mound of forget-me-nots where she discovered the golden locket that launched the whole adventure.

After Germaine pointed out these garden landmarks, she pulled another piece of paper from a pocket and smoothed it out on the old wooden worktable. "And this was in the tree, too. I'm only showing it to you because I know you will treat it confidentially."

Leonora Parker read the letter and looked at her client. "Germaine," she said, "if you show this letter to Aubrey Bowles, maybe he'll let the whole thing drop."

"Leonora," Germaine answered, "you don't know Aubrey Bowles. Besides, it was Miss Rose's express wish that he not be told. His father and his aunt, Aubrey Two and Viola Bowles, were very dear to Rose's memory, and she didn't want to do anything to besmirch their good names. One imagines she never met this cousin, yet her wishes must be obeyed."

By the time Leonora Parker and Germaine had returned to the parlor, the photographer had arrived. Sheriff Archer and Chauncey were finishing up their inventory and seemed to have become quite cordial during their task.

"Germaine, did you know that the sheriff spends his summers painting in the Hudson Valley, and that's why he is so well-acquainted with the work of Thompson and Church?" Chauncey asked.

"How very interesting," Germaine responded before turning to Leonora who was returning the documentation to the sheriff.

"Well Germaine, I'm sorry, but you will have to comply with this court order. You are to turn over the jewelry, the box, and the will that was in the box to the sheriff. You say you don't know anything about the haberdashery collection, and I don't really think that will be questioned by the complainants. The stocks and bonds that are referred to in the newly-discovered will were distributed in keeping with the terms of the earlier will. Reassigning those will be up to the courts. However," she said, turning now to the sheriff, "my client is well within her rights to retain the property until she is satisfied that the inventory you and Mr. Fetterson have undertaken is complete. And I advise her to retain the property until the photographs your office took are developed.

"That way," she said, looking first at Germaine, then at the sheriff, "we will know if any pieces are missing when the collection is turned over to the museum." The sheriff agreed to the attorney's terms, and sent the photographer back to headquarters with orders to develop the pictures immediately and to make three copies of each image.

Germaine thought that Sheriff Archer and Attorney Parker might enjoy a tour of the garden, and as she led them outside, she asked Andrew McGrath to show the visitors what he had done so far. The constables stood warily by the side of the shed, wondering what was taking their boss so long to execute what seemed to them a routine task. Germaine excused herself and asked Chauncey to join her inside for a moment. Once inside, Germaine asked Chauncey to phone Helen and explain the situation to her. While he did so, Germaine ran into the library and gathered up the sisters' letters, the note that was in the tree, and the newspaper articles about the Swarthy Swiper. She silently made her way towards the back stairs, which had no windows, and thus allowed her to go to the basement unseen. When she got to the basement, she tucked all the papers into the secret compartment beside the fireplace ash collector. When she was done, she tiptoed up the back stairs and returned to the library. She had just sat down at the library desk when the Sheriff and Attorney Parker knocked on the open door to the room to announce their arrival.

"May we come in?" Leonora asked.

"Oh certainly," Germaine responded as calmly as she could, having just caught her breath. "I was just gathering up the various copies of the Sheppard, Santini, and Bowles wills, and was putting them together with the newly discovered final will of

Miss Rose." She smiled. "I thought it would make it easier to sort all this out if all the documents were in one place."

Leonora said, "That is very generous of you, Germaine. So like you always to think of others before yourself." Germaine only smiled in response. Sheriff Archer had noticed that Germaine was slightly out of breath, but he said nothing.

"Did you enjoy your tour of the garden?" she asked the two visitors. They agreed that they had. "I think young Andrew McGrath has done a wonderful job. He has a real talent for historic gardening. Perhaps he'll go on to study it in college," she mused, leading the others back downstairs.

The photographer was standing in the entry vestibule, three large manila envelopes in hand. "Here you are, Sir," he said to Sheriff Archer. "I had the boys in the darkroom do a rush job, just like you asked." And he handed the sheriff all three sets of photos. Attorney Parker insisted that the sheriff and she review the photos together to ensure that the three sets were identical. The dining room seemed like the best place to do this, so Mrs. White cleared the simple blue and white Myson plates which she had laid on the table for Germaine's lunch before all the commotion started, and the two got down to work.

At last, the attorney was satisfied that all the photographs were the same. Only then would she allow the sheriff to take the jewels and the copies of the wills. "My client is clearly in the right here, Sheriff," she said. "Those items should go straight to the Historical Society." Sheriff Archer shrugged his shoulders as if to say it was beyond his control.

"When do you go before the judge?" she asked.

"As soon as I leave here. I'm going to straight to Judge Adams' chambers with all of this," he replied.

"I'm going with you. I bet Bowles will have some fancy lawyer from Boston there. I want to make sure my client has representation," Leonora Parker said sternly.

"You are very welcome. Would you like to come with me in my car?" he asked. She thought she could keep an eye on him that way, so she agreed. The two drove off in the Sheriff's car, followed by the two constables and the jewels in a patrol car. The men were very relieved to sit down after hours of standing in the hot sun out in the garden. As they drove off, Helen came around the corner and waved to her friends.

"What's all that about?" she asked, motioning to the two official vehicles that were disappearing down Beaumont Street.

"Mrs. White finally lost control of herself and strangled the mailman," Chauncey joked about the long-standing enmity between the housekeeper and the mailman.

"I just might one day," Mrs. White said, overhearing Chauncey's jest. "So will it be the three of you for lunch and a plate in the kitchen for the McGrath boy?" she asked. The friends both indicated they could stay for lunch, so Mrs. White re-set the table and soon brought out a hearty spread of omelets, salad, and freshly baked bread.

"Mrs. White, you've outdone yourself," Chauncey said, contentedly patting his stomach as she came in to clear the dishes.

"It's a pleasure making lunch for you three young'uns," she said warmly. "I like it when the house is full with your chatter. Much better than having all those policemen hanging about.

"I expect that lady lawyer of yours to make short work of that Aubrey Bowles, Germaine," she went on. "I've never cared for him. His mum Viola was a dear and his father Aubrey Junior was a kind, gentle sort of man, but this one and his brother Hugo are simply not to be trusted."

"I don't know, Hugo has done some good deeds in his day," Germaine said, reminding the others about how he saved Bowles, Incorporated after Aubrey had nearly brought it to ruin.

"I'm with Mrs. White," Helen said. "Neither one is to be trusted. Now that we've finished eating, will you please tell me how Aubrey Bowles got involved in all this, and why on earth he sent the sheriff over here?"

"You two help Mrs. White clear, and I'll explain everything over tea," Germaine said, excusing herself from the room. She first went up to the library and picked up the extra copies of the family wills she had copied at the probate clerk's office. Then she headed to the basement, taking the front stairs this time, and carefully removed all the documents which she had hastily stashed in the hidden compartment when the sheriff and his men were there. She re-entered the dining room with arms full of papers and files.

"You're a one-woman filing cabinet, Germaine. Let me take some of those," Chauncey said, helping his friend unburden herself of the paperwork. She spread it out carefully on the table in chronological order.

"Here are the letters between Lucetta and Philippa," she said, indicating a pile of aged envelopes. "Here are the newspaper articles about the Swarthy Swiper," she pointed to the next pile. "These are copies of the Sheppard family wills, Lyman Sheppard, who was Lucetta and Philippa's father, here, and Edith Sheppard, Lyman's second wife and the girls' mother," this as she tapped a stack of thick legal documents. "Here are the wills of Philippa and Lorenzo Santini, and here are the wills of Colonel Aubrey Bowles, Lucetta Sheppard Bowles, Viola Bowles Smith and Aubrey Bowles Junior," this last was quite a towering pile. "And this pile here," she said, pointing to the largest compilation of all, "houses *all* the wills of Miss Rose, starting from when she was only fifteen to when she died at ninety-two. The will from her ninety-second year was the one we found in the empty jewelry box, and it is a binding legal document that should supersede all previous ones.

"But," she went on, "one of the previous ones names the heirs of the Bowles family – namely the children of Viola Bowles Newton and Aubrey Bowles Junior as her heirs. So the Bowles people can, and I think will, challenge the legitimacy of something handwritten on a piece of paper versus something official looking and drawn up in a lawyer's office."

"But her last will was witnessed by Jebidiah Sharpe, who was a widely respected judge," Helen said, examining Germaine's copy of the document which the sheriff had taken away.

"That's what I hope will work in our favor," Germaine replied. "When Judge Adams sees that Judge Sharpe witnessed the will, he should just dismiss any previous wills. Let's cross our fingers that he sees it that way."

Chapter Twenty Six: Back to work

As the trio awaited word from the attorney, Germaine told Helen everything that had happened in the past few days, from seeing Pugsy meet with Aubrey Bowles to following A.B. Three into the newspaper office. "I think Miss Rose realized that she didn't want to hurt the Bowles family's reputation the way her own father's reputation had been harmed, so she changed the will. I imagine she thought the jewels were better off in the hands of a museum so that the public could enjoy them and no private person would covet them and do evil deeds in pursuit of them."

"But how on earth did she get the jewels into the tree at ninety-two years old," Chauncey asked in disbelief. "Andrew McGrath showed us where you found the jewels, and that's very high up!"

"Well, from all accounts she was pretty spry. She rowed her canoe up and down the river every day until she was eightly," Germaine answered. "But she might have had help," she conceded.

As the three friends pondered the image of a nonagenarian climbing up an eight-foot ladder, the telephone rang. Germaine ran into the hall to answer it. Her friends didn't follow, but did strain to hear her end of the conversation.

All they could hear was "Oh, I am so pleased!" After a few moments, Germaine returned to her friends smiling radiantly. "That was Leonora Parker. The judge admitted the final will, since it was signed by Jebediah Sharpe. He suggested that Aubrey brush up on the law if he *does* become a senator, and he ordered the sheriff to deliver the jewels to the Historical Society today. He said I could gather up the journals this week, and he said if the hats were not found, they were not found, but if they ever turned up, they were to be given to the Historical Society upon discovery."

"Oh, Germaine, that's wonderful!" Helen said as Chauncey nodded in agreement.

"But wait until you hear the next part," she said, pausing dramatically before going on.

"Germaine!" Chauncey chided.

"Okay, okay. The stocks and bonds — Aubrey has to donate the value of the stocks and bonds that he inherited from Miss Rose to the Historic Society. The judge ordered Leonora to research it, and she thinks it's close to a million dollars!"

"Wow! The Historical Society will never have to do fundraising again," Helen said, thinking about the least pleasant aspect of her beloved job.

"I'm going to telephone the chairman of the board of trustees right now," Germaine announced.

Germaine, Helen, and Chauncey drove over to the chairman's house to explain the good news. He hardly knew what to say, but thanked the young people profusely. As they were celebrating their good fortune, Sheriff Archer drove up with the jewels and the chest. He told the chairman that he would be happy to keep the jewelry in safe storage at the jail if the museum wasn't ready to display the precious items just yet. Germaine suggested the museum consult Edward Bartlett on the best display. Everyone decided that was a good idea, and the chairman shook the young people's hands repeatedly.

"Oh Miss Moreau," he said, "We are already so grateful to you for the donations you give us from your decorating work and now this. I hardly know how to thank you." There was a tear in his eye.

"Just displaying the jewels is thanks enough, Mr. Stephenson," Germaine said. "Knowing the public will be able to see these amazing works of art is a wonderful feeling." The three friends left, and drove together to Germaine's house.

"Just think, Germaine," Helen said, "this all started with you digging in the garden and finding a locket. Who would ever have thought that you would have uncovered the true identity of the Swarthy Swiper and then have had to cover it back up, never mind that you would discover a huge treasure of jewels in a tree, and carry out Miss Rose's final wishes. It's been quite a journey!"

"If only I could find the hats, then I could feel I'd really wrapped things up," Germaine said with a smile. "I'm so glad I could help carry out a wonderful woman's last wishes."

The young friends telephoned Edward Bartlett to catch him up on the news, and Germaine asked if he would help with the display of the Russian jewel chest and the jewels at the museum. He was pleased to oblige the request.

"There's one thing I can't figure out, though," said Helen. "Who had the word *wronged* engraved on Lorenzo Santini's headstone? Was it Miss Rose?"

"I can't prove it, but I believe it was. The cemetery caretaker said no one knew how it got there, but judging from the font and the depth of the engraving, I believe Rose Santini did it to right her father's reputation in some small way. She's buried beside him," Germaine answered.

At last, the friends all went their separate ways, and Germaine turned to the pile of correspondence that had amassed in the last few days. She chose a local project that she hoped to help with, the identification and restoration of the original fresco design at Ventforth Hall, a stately home in the nearby Berkshires. Just as she finished up her paperwork, Mrs. White came in to tell her that Andrew McGrath had finished the garden and wanted to show it to her. She picked something up off the desk and went outside.

The garden was superb. It looked just as it had when the Sheppards originally designed it in the Victorian era.

"Andrew, you've outdone yourself!" Germaine exclaimed.

"You're a good lad," said Mrs. White. "You know the value of an honest day's work, now, don't you?"

"Yes, ma'am," Andrew answered sincerely. Then he turned to Germaine Moreau. "Miss Germaine, do you really like it?" he asked timidly.

"I love it, Andrew. You've done a fine job, and if you ever need a reference, I will be pleased to tell anyone what good work you have done," she smiled.

"I'm going to use some of my earnings to take a class at the Historical Society," he said. "My grandfather said I could. I learned so much out here, and I just want to learn even more. I want to find out all about that arrowhead."

"Do you still have it in your pocket, Andrew?" Germaine asked. He nodded.

"Well, I don't know that it's the safest place for it, so I've got a box you might like to keep it in," said Germaine, pulling the sterling snuff box that Andrew unearthed from her pocket. "I think the arrowhead will fit nicely in this," she said, handing it to the boy.

"Can I really have it?" Andrew McGrath stammered.

"Yes. I've cleaned it up for you, but it's up to you to research the history of it, and to treasure it," Germaine said, smiling.

Mrs. White raised an eyebrow at what she thought was an extravagant show of thanks for the young boy, but said nothing. She thought that Germaine was generous to a fault.

"Now make sure that Littleton boy doesn't set his beady little eyes on it," she said.

"Where is Pugsy, Andrew?" asked Germaine. I haven't seen him around lately.

"Oh, he's in big trouble," Andrew said. "He tried to steal something at one of the shops downtown, and when the cops picked him up, he had a thousand dollars in his pocket. He refused to say where he got all that money, and they sent him to reform school."

"That's where he belongs," said Mrs. White, crossing her arms.

"I hope that he can change his ways," Germaine said sadly. "When he gets out," she said, turning towards Andrew McGrath, "I hope he'll see the life you are choosing by working hard and studying. Maybe he will see that there is a different way."

Germaine was very busy with research for her next big project over the next several days, and when a small package arrived in the mail, she was sure it was related to her fresco work. She was quite surprised when she opened it to find that it was a golden locket; a replica of the one she found in the garden, but with her initials, and with photos of her parents inside. It was inscribed *In grateful appreciation from the Springdale Historical Society* on the back. A very kind note was in the package, signed by each member of the board of trustees. Germaine smiled as she closed the clasp of the necklace and admired it in the mirror.

And with that, she went back to work.

The end.